THE BODY CATCHER

The Body Catcher

MEGAN DERR

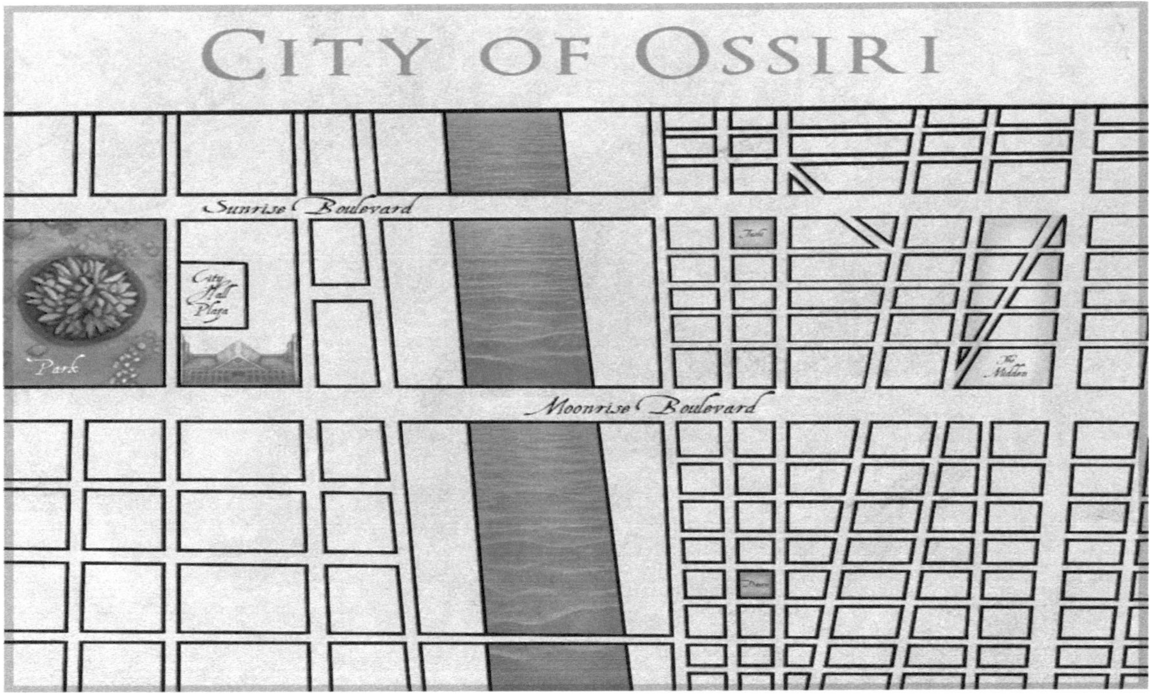

CITY OF OSSIRI
Sunrise Boulevard
Moonrise Boulevard
City Hall Plaza
Park
The Madison

Chapter One

Tashi finished sewing up the coarse burlap, knotting the thread and bending to cut it with his teeth, since he'd lost his scissors at some point and hadn't yet been able to replace them.

Tucking his tools away, he drew a quick cantrip in the air for lightness, cast it over the burlap-wrapped body weighted with rocks, and shoved it into the murky depths of the River Oss, canceling the cantrip as he did so. The body vanished quickly, and the lime he'd used would help ensure it didn't rise if something went wrong with the burlap and rocks.

As jobs went, this was one of the few he didn't really mind. Abusive bastards fueled exclusively by booze and dubious powders were seldom missed by anyone. Child's play to dispose of, and there was rarely more than a perfunctory obituary posted. Easy money, and the abuse victims got to live without being afraid every moment of every day.

Making sure the area was clear, with no trace of his shenanigans left behind, Tashi headed off to collect payment.

The night air was pleasantly chilly, the last dregs of winter fighting bitterly against spring's firm grasp. He loved spring weather, but he hated the increase in people it brought. The more people about at late hours, the more difficult his job.

At least he was never short of work. In Eastbridge, the poor half of the city, there was always somebody who needed a body disposed of.

The bell at city hall was tolling the second hour as he reached Lime Street. Despite its name, the businesses here processed a lot more than lime, though lime and lye made up the majority of it. People were more than happy to pay him in both or allow him to purchase large quantities of them, no questions asked.

Slipping down an alleyway, he kept on past several houses until he came to the one he'd visited just a couple of hours ago. A lamp still glowed in the kitchen window. He rapped on the door, tugging down his hood to be certain all was safely hidden. The door opened ever so slightly, part of a pale face just barely visible. "It's done."

"Thank you," the woman whispered, and slipped a few coins into his palm. Thirty cols, more than enough to tide him over for a few weeks.

The door closed and he went back the way he'd come, tucking the coins away in a pocket that thieves couldn't reach.

All in all, a pretty good night, and it was only two in the morning. He could grab a bite to eat from one of the late shops and read for a bit before going to sleep.

About a block from his house, he stepped into a shop for his favorite fish and chips, but his hopes for a quiet, pleasant couple of hours before bed were dashed as he spied a figure waiting on the landing just a couple of steps from his door.

"No," he said as he drew close enough to identify the figure. "I don't care what it is or how much it pays, I'm not doing it." He unlocked his door and stepped inside, sighing long and loud and pointed when Dawa followed him inside. "No means no."

Dawa shut the door and shoved back his hood, sending his gold-brown curls flying in about fifty directions. His brown skin seemed to absorb the meager light as Tashi snapped his fingers to light his lamps. "Please, Tashi. I wouldn't come if it wasn't important."

"You always say that, and you always get me into worlds of trouble."

"Please, I am begging you. I am blood

desperate, Tashi. *Please.*"

That drew Tashi up short. Dawa was more superstitious than a fortune-telling sailor; he would never use such a term lightly. Setting his food down and removing his own hood and face mask, Tashi said, "What in the names of the Seven is going on?"

"It's not me," Dawa said, stepping further into the room, enough the lamps flickered in his brown eyes, making them almost gold in flashes. "I dare not say too much aloud, but you have to come. You're the only one who can do it."

Tashi groaned and sat down, burying his fingers in his hair, heavy and thick, sweaty and messy after a long night's work. Damn it all, he'd just wanted peace and quiet for once. "What happens if I refuse?"

"A lot of people are going to die. *A lot.* I'm not talking five or ten or even twenty. I mean hundreds, all of them from the Rotter."

"Dawa, what in the Eternal Night have you gotten yourself into?"

The night only grew more baffling as Dawa started to cry—and clearly he'd been holding back the tears for some time, given the force at which they came out. "We were trying to save them. Seven grant us mercy, we just wanted to save them."

Them. Tashi's heart sank. Given what Dawa did for a living, *them* only ever meant one thing. A mother and child who'd not survived the birthing. Damn it. Damn everything.

Righting his mask and hood, Tashi pushed to his feet. "Let's go, then." Dawa burst into fresh tears and hugged him tightly. Tashi sighed and untangled him. "Come on."

"Thank you," Dawa whispered, and led the way out of the room as he pulled up his hood.

Tashi locked his door, double-checked the protection cantrip was still in place, and followed Dawa down the stairs and back out into the night.

This time, they headed in the opposite direction of the way he'd come home, far from the grungy streets of the poor and working classes and toward the tidier streets that were the domain of the middle class… and then, ominously, onward still, across the bridge into the wealthy part of the city known as Westbridge, on and on until they were in one of the wealthy neighborhoods. Swan Lake, in fact, where everyone was related to some royal or another, if not actually royalty.

Whatever Dawa was dragging him into this time, if even one thing went wrong, people were definitely going to die. Fuck, fuck, *fuck*.

Tashi couldn't even bring himself to make a tasteless joke about having plenty of work.

His stomach sank as they stopped in front a large, sprawling house painted dark blue with white and gray accents. He didn't need light to know this house. Nobody did. "What have you done?" he hissed. "You don't make house calls."

"We did for this one," Dawa replied with a world-weary sigh. "This way." He slipped down the narrow passage between the blue house and its neighbor. Thorny hedges scraped against them as they walked, and their footsteps echoed despite every care to remain silent.

Tashi hated this part of town. He stayed as far away as he possibly could, and only rarely accepted work that brought him here. The last job he'd taken had been more than a year ago. The less he had to do with rich people, the happier he was.

As they reached the back of the house, Dawa drew out a key and unlocked the pedestrian gate, which creaked quietly, thankfully, as he opened and closed it. They headed off across the courtyard, so eerily empty and still at that hour, when during the day it would be bustling with deliveries, servants, and more, such a vital part of the house, tied to the kitchen that was the heart, and the owners did not appreciate it one wit.

Inside, they crept through the kitchen into the servant quarters. Strange. People weren't usually in danger over the death of a servant. Usually the nobles paid off the family and everybody went on with their day.

He wished fervently that he'd been able to throw Dawa out, instead of yet again giving in to his pleading.

Dawa came to a stop at the second to last door on the hall and rapped twice, then three more times. There was some shuffling inside, rattling as the door was unlocked, and then it was opened by a pale-skinned woman with eyes puffy and face red from crying. "You're back, thank the Seven."

"I brought him," Dawa said softly. "As promised. He'll help, as best anyone can."

The woman nodded and stood back to let them in.

The room smelled of blood, and death rubbed against his skin like coarse fabric or sandpaper.

He crossed the room to the dead figure, absently noting the fine silk and linen clothes that had been carefully set aside before the birthing had begun. Someone had draped a sheet over the poor woman, and Tashi gently pulled it away from her face. His rule was usually to know as little as possible, but this time he had a sinking feeling he needed to know the face beneath the sheet.

Whatever he'd expected—noblewoman, a well-kept mistress, famous actress—it was not to see the frozen-in-pain face of Princess Safir, youngest daughter of the queen, third in line for the throne, widowed at just twenty, and set to remarry in just nine more months. She was so thin, so wasted away, that he barely recognized her. Only twenty-four, but she looked so much older. Why?

For that matter, why in the world had she been pregnant? That wasn't just a scandal, that could destroy the pending engagement and years of peace... He was surprised the queen had allowed her to carry the babe to term.

No wonder Dawa was so stressed.

Replacing the sheet, Tashi turned to Dawa and the woman. "What in the *Eternal Night* is going on?"

Dawa's mouth pinched as he stared at the sheet-draped corpse. "To be honest, I don't know much of anything. One of her maids approached me months ago. I scarcely believed a word of what she was saying to me, but she arranged a meeting and everything. We worked out the details. She couldn't risk going all the way to our offices, so we arranged to tend the matter here."

"How did she die?" Tashi asked. "I mean, besides the obvious. She doesn't look like she was strong enough to carry a baby, let alone birth it."

Anger filled the woman's face. Tashi didn't recognize her, so she must be Dawa's newest assistant. They tended not to last long. "She never should have been pregnant in the first place. She was weak, sickly; the pregnancy was killing her. They should have ended the matter before it became a problem, and gotten a surrogate mother for health purposes if producing a child was so damn important."

"Princess Safir should have been in good health. She's a *princess*, for Night's sake."

Snorting, the woman said, "Illness doesn't give a damn about rank."

"No, but the queen and other members of the family should have."

"I can't tell you why they didn't, only that it's clear from the state of the body that her health has been declining steadily the past few years. Disease, neglect, or something else entirely, I couldn't begin to guess, but she wasn't strong enough to take care of herself, let alone have a baby."

"I'm sorry to drag you into this," Dawa said. "Especially after you've already done so much for me. For us. Believe it or not, I do try my damnedest not to burden you with my problems. It's just that in this case, I didn't know who else to trust. We can't return the body to the palace, or else…"

Or else the queen would tear apart the entire city, one body at a time, to find someone to blame for the deaths of her daughter and grandchild. Her reaction to them going missing would not be much better, but she couldn't burn anything down until she had answers.

As a stopgap, it would have to do, and Seven protect whoever got stuck figuring out the permanent solution.

"It's fine," he replied. "I mean, it's not, but I understand the lose-lose situation. No matter what we do, the city is going to be torn apart. But if they never know what happened, fewer people will die." He cupped Dawa's cheek, brushing away tears, and kissed the opposite one. "Leave me to my work, now. You can clean up when I'm done."

Dawa nodded, motioned to the nearby woman, and together they hastily left the room.

Leaving Tashi alone with two corpses, a situation he'd been in more times than he could count now. He turned up every light in the room, giving him as much light as possible to work in without having to draw upon magic for it.

Discarding his cape, hood, and mask, he rolled up the sleeves of his shirt and set to work. A body like this would have to be buried. He preferred the river for most of his work, but something like this, the chance something could go wrong and the body float to the surface was too great.

Bodies. There were two, as much as he hated to think about it. Children were always the worst. He hated burying children. Thankfully, such grisly work was extremely rare.

Returning to the body, he removed the sheet entirely, casting it to the far side of the body and well out of his way. Someone, likely Dawa, had placed the baby in her arms. A little girl, who probably would have been every bit like her mother. The royal family of the queendom of Valithta had always boasted fierce women.

Which made this entire situation all the stranger. Thankfully, it wasn't his problem. Only this sad, grim duty fell to him. The fallout was for somebody else to deal with.

He tended the baby first, wrapping it gently in a tiny, crocheted blanket it had not lived long enough to enjoy, then in a strip of sheet that he'd affix to his chest as a sling. Her Highness was a bit more tricky, but a few cantrips and some muscle and he got her secured in a bundle he could strap to his back. After that it was only a matter of a few more cantrips and then getting everything into place.

With his cargo secured, he headed out. When he was across the courtyard and back in the narrow passage between houses, he cast the last, most vital and dangerous cantrip. It faded him from view, persuaded eyes to skip over him.

It was also illegal without a special license, which he very much did not have. Not anymore. He would face a great deal more trouble if he was caught transporting a body, though, nevermind the bodies of a royal princess and her newborn.

Sighing, he slipped out onto the street and started the long journey across Westbridge, over the bridges back to Eastbridge, and onward to a place so derelict even the most desperate, depraved criminals avoided going there. The Old City, it was called, destroyed and razed nearly two centuries ago, the poisonous magic involved in that war so brutal that even now the land was barren, black, completely unusable. Nothing remained but ruins, the scorched skeleton that had once been known as the Crown of the World.

He continued on until he came to what was

barely identifiable as a temple. It was still a lousy place to discard a woman and child like so much trash, but it was moderately better than his other options. At least he liked to think so.

Setting the bodies carefully aside, using more magic to undo the tight bundle he'd reduced Princess Safir to in order to get her there, he headed off to his stash. He might not bury bodies often, but he was always prepared should it be necessary.

A short distance away, in the remains of a building that had been an office or house, he could never entirely tell which, he tossed aside old strips of wood and bits of stone until he uncovered the bags of lye and lime he kept there, along with digging supplies. A few cantrips and the heavy bags moved easily, the shovel stacked on top of them.

Back at the temple, he set the bags down, grabbed the shovel, and set to work. Thankfully, the ground was soft, easy to dig up, the smell earthy and loamy, surprisingly pleasant for such a foul, depressing area. Perhaps there was yet sanctity left in the old temple.

When the hole was dug, he covered the bottom with generous measures of lye and lime. One to speed rotting, the other to contend with the gases and odors, which would also help speed the process. After that was done, he used another cantrip to gently place mother and child inside. Now for the part he really didn't want to do.

Dropping into the hole, he pulled the knife at his waist and started slicing—abdomen, up the chest as much as he could, being certain to cut up organs as he went. It left him bloody and smelly and filthy, and wanting to throw up, but it was this or let hundreds of people die.

When the job was done, he cleaned his hands as best he could and reached out to cup one of Princess Safir's cheeks. Only then did he let the anguish and remorse run through him, tears dripping down his cheeks before he wiped them impatiently away.

As he stood, a gleam of gold from his torch caught his eye, and he crouched again, brushing away strands of hair. How had he missed it before?

A necklace, gleaming gold set with a sapphire pendant. He gingerly picked it up, fingers seeking the hidden catch.

Inside the secret locket was a piece of paper that had been folded many times to fit, and a tiny portrait of two children, one five years old, the other just barely three at the time.

Closing the locket, Tashi sought the closure on the necklace and, after a couple of failed tries, managed to open it. He tucked the necklace into the secret pocket that held his coins, then finally climbed out of the grave. He covered the bodies with more lime and lye, more than enough to do the deed, and then set to filling it, tamping the earth down as he went, and scattering what was left to hide the grave was there at all.

When the deed was finally done, and no sign of Princess Safir and her daughter remained, Tashi put his shovel away, slung his satchel back across his chest, and wiped sweat from his face with his last clean handkerchief.

Standing over the grave as the sky just barely began to hint at dawn, he said, "May you find peace and joy in the gardens of Eternal Day, little sister, and never again know the pain of this life. Farewell."

Wiping a few more errant tears away, Tashi headed back into the city and home, this time hopefully to remain there until he had to go to work once more.

Thankfully, he passed no one except some apathetic guards eager to sign out and find their beds, and some drunks who would likely be sleeping in whatever gutter they fell into shortly. He trudged up the stairs to his flat, thoughts on a cup of the good tea he saved for nights like this before he climbed into bed and slept all day—and stopped halfway there.

His door was just barely ajar.

Not only had someone picked the lock, they'd also disabled his protection cantrip.

Fuck this entire stupid night.

Chapter Two

As much as he would prefer to avoid whatever mess was waiting for him now, he didn't have the energy for a game of hide and seek, so with a long sigh he pushed the door all the way open and stepped inside.

His heart dropped into his stomach as he took in the man sitting at his rickety table. Dark skin, close-cropped goatee, multiple earrings, more piercings in his nose, chin, and eyebrows. Handsome, in a fierce, sharp cut sort of way. He would be nearly fifty by now, and time had only made him more compelling and attractive than ever. Tashi wouldn't have expected otherwise, if he'd ever allowed himself to think about it. About him.

Rumér, his mentor since Tashi had been old enough to start mage training. He was one of the most renowned mages in the world, and the most famous mage in Valishta. He could have been Warlock Prime to Queen Rasha, but had never wanted to take on such a bond. When Tashi had been forced to leave, Rumér and Safir had been the only ones who'd come to tell him goodbye, the only ones who'd seemed like they would genuinely miss him.

There was far too much of his past cropping up tonight. First the sister he'd loved most, and now this old heartache.

Closing the door and locking it, Tashi then finally removed his hood, mask, and cloak, hanging everything on the hooks by the door before pushing further into the small room he called home. Once upon a time, his bathing chamber had been twice the size of this room, nevermind the size of his entire royal flat.

That room, that life, seemed like something from a dream. Something that belonged to someone else. Which, it did really. Prince Tenzin Kuliri Hashar, on track to have been Warlock Prime to Crown Princess Janashta one day, was long dead.

Tashi was all that remained, and Tashi wanted to go to bed and mourn his sister, not deal with more ghosts.

"It's been a long time, Tenzin. I was always surprised you chose to remain in the city. I would have thought you'd get as far away as possible."

"That requires money, or doing things I won't stoop to," Tashi said coldly. "You'll recall Her Majesty tossed me out with barely the clothes on my back. I think she hoped I'd be killed by a thief or whoever I prostituted myself to first. She always did enjoy that she could make everyone else do her dirty work. My name is Tashi. What do you want, Warlock?"

Rumér flinched, but only said, "Tashi then, my apologies. I know you don't want to see me, see any of us, and I wouldn't bother you if it wasn't important."

"Let's have it, then, so I can tell you no and throw you out."

"Your mother is dying."

Tashi drew up short. He'd expected Rumér to tell him about Safir, ask if he'd seen her. Not… not this.

There was entirely too much family drama happening, especially considering he wasn't part of the family anymore, and hadn't been for a long time. Shoving back the tumult, he said coolly, "Am I supposed to care? She made her feelings about me pretty damn clear twelve years ago. Don't expect me to care about her now."

"I wouldn't," Rumér said quietly. "The problem is vastly more complicated than that."

Tashi sighed and went to fix some tea, since

it was clear he wouldn't be getting to sleep any time soon. "It's also not *my* problem. I have plenty of sisters who should be handling the matter, whatever it is. Why are you bothering me?"

"Because I don't think it's natural. I don't even think it's poison. I think it's a curse."

"So break it," Tashi said, even though it couldn't be that easy if Rumér had bothered to track him down. Pouring tea into a badly chipped mug, he sat at the rickety table. It was small enough that he could smell Rumér's vanilla-cinnamon cologne, the flowery incense of the palace. He could reach out and touch if he wanted, but he wasn't that stupid. Even if they weren't now leagues apart in life, even if Tashi was still a prince and warlock, Rumér would never see him as anything but a student, the difference in their ages.

Not that it mattered, because Tashi wasn't going to complicate his life by doing something that stupid. He'd been doing just fine with the occasional whore, thanks. The fewer attachments in his life, the better. He'd learned that lesson hard, but he'd learned it well.

"I can't find it," Rumér said.

"What do you mean *you* can't find it." Tashi abandoned his tea. "What do you mean you *can't find* it? I don't even know which part of that statement is the strangest."

Rumér stole his tea, and it was hard not to notice the beautiful dark teal he'd painted his nails. Tashi had always loved the attention Rumér gave his nails, how much he enjoyed painting them, even sometimes adding small jewels and the like. Rumér was generally stoic, straightforward, but he loved his jewelry and painting his nails.

"I mean it's an extremely high-level curse, anchored somewhere in the city and heavily obscured."

"For a curse to work at a distance like that, it would require some of her blood." Tashi drummed his fingers on the table. Royal blood was not easily obtained, but a few bribes in the right places and anything could be accomplished. Especially when very few of the staff liked his mother, unless a miracle had happened since he'd left. "You want me to find it. Why should I?"

"Because I don't know who is responsible for it yet, and whoever is killing your mother might just go for your sisters next. You might not care about your mother, and fair enough, but what about Safir? She—"

"Safir is dead," Tashi said flatly. He hadn't planned on revealing that tidbit, but the curse had changed all that. "She died in childbirth just hours ago. I buried her myself." He withdrew the pendant he'd taken from her and dropped it on the table. "Explain to me why my little sister was half-dead already, pregnant, and unmarried."

Rumér sighed, looking tired and old. "She would never reveal the father's identity, never confirmed anything but that it was consensual. From what little I was able to glean, and from watching her, I think her lover was a feral. I think the babe was feral as well, and slowly leeched more of her life than her body could endure. I assume the babe died as well?"

"Yes."

"Damn it." Rumér rubbed his temples with one hand, then let his hand fall. "I'll handle it. Where is she buried?"

"Old City," Tashi replied, and gave sufficient landmarks, though he doubted anyone would be retrieving the body. "Do you have any idea at all who the father could have been?"

"I have some suspicions, and I'll have a name before the week is out, do not worry," Rumér said darkly.

"Then I'm happy to let you handle the matter. Night knows I never wanted to," Tashi replied, relieved the problem had been lifted, and happy that Safir would have justice. "Just leave Eastbridge out of it, nobody here did anything except what Safir paid them to do." He picked the locket up and tucked it into his pocket again. What he would do with the damned thing, he didn't know, but fool that he was, he felt a little better having a piece of her with him.

She was the only one of them who didn't deserve such a cruel fate, but there was fuck-all he could do about it now, and better Rumér dealt with it than the former prince who'd been thrown out and left to die.

"So what do you want from me?" he asked, even though he already knew the answer.

"Find that curse. Your skills were near to surpassing mine before… before everything… I have every faith you are well past me by now. Find the curse and break it. Gather whatever information you can."

"How should I get it to you?"

"I'll come to you every few days," Rumér replied. "If I can't, I'll send a message. Be careful, Tashi."

Tashi laughed. "I live in the slums—have for the past twelve years. I've faced thieves, thugs, would-be rapists, and more. My neighbors are violent criminals or violent people who haven't been caught yet. I'm a body catcher now, not a soft, spoiled prince. I'll find your Night-damned curse, but only so I can go back to being left alone."

Rumér stared at him, sadness in his eyes and every line of his face. "I fought for you, Tashi. I fought so hard that she nearly banished me. I have tried all these years to get her to reverse her decision, and I keep aware of you so I can find you should that day ever come."

"I don't need saving, and I don't need nor want to go back. That's not my life anymore." Sometimes he wondered if it ever really had been.

Sighing, Rumér said, "Well, be careful anyway. One more thing…"

"What?"

"Princess Sha-wen is coming to visit at the beginning of next month. I think your mother is meant to be dead by then. Work quickly."

"Go away."

Rumér looked as though he wanted to say more, but thankfully he only nodded and left, closing the door quietly and easily resetting Tashi's protections.

Sha-wen. There was a name he'd never expected to hear again. They'd been betrothed since they were children—him ten, her twelve. She'd been his first sexual encounter, when they'd met just after his seventeenth birthday. He'd learned quickly he had a particular fondness for beautiful women who couldn't be bothered to disrobe, simply gathered up their fancy skirts out of the way before fucking him right there on the floor of his private parlor. She'd taught him much—kissing, fucking, sucking her delightful cock.

One more ghost to haunt him, one more life he would no longer live. Why was she visiting? To marry one of his sisters instead? That seemed likely.

Ignoring the sting of bile in his throat, he drank what remained of the tea, gone ice cold now, then shucked his boots and most of his clothes and climbed into bed.

~~*

He woke a few hours later to sunshine, a rare sight in Ossiri City, an even rarer sight for a body catcher.

Tashi sighed as the previous night washed over him, pinching his eyes against the tears that wanted out. Tears were useless. He'd cried his eyes out, begged until he was hoarse, made a fucking *fool* of himself, and still his mother had thrown him out like so much trash. *You should be grateful I'm not executing you like I should.*

Shaking the memories off, he rose—and stopped as something clattered to the floor. He looked down, then stooped and retrieved the locket. Hadn't he left it in his cloak? Whatever. Flicking the catch, he stared at the images inside: Safir and their cousin Rashtu as small children. The two had been as close as siblings, if not closer.

Rashtu had fallen ill not six months after the portrait was painted, though, and not recovered despite the efforts of at least ten healers. The first of many tragedies endured by their family. Tashi's great and terrible crime and subsequent expulsion had almost been relaxing by comparison.

Sighing softly, Tashi secured the necklace around his own neck. Sentimental drivel, but if he left it in his flat, someone would eventually find a way to steal it.

There was a long day ahead of him, so first thing first: a good meal that would see him through until morning, since once he got to work, there'd be little to no chance to stop.

He pulled on clean clothes, threw his dirty ones in the hamper he'd have to take to his laundress tomorrow, and finally pulled on cloak, hood, and mask. Stepping into the hallway, he secured his door with key and magic, and headed off to face his day.

Downstairs in the lobby, the first order of business was his mailbox. Not actually his, this was an empty one the landlord let him use with no questions asked, for the odd assistance here and there with tenants who died inconveniently.

The box had two slips of paper, so his evening was already looking to be busy. He tucked them away to read later and headed out into the day. Sunshine always brought out the full force of the awful smells that permeated the slums, but he couldn't be bothered to care when there was actual sunshine warming him, even if he couldn't feel it on his skin the way he wished.

He headed down the street to the main intersection, already bustling with hawkers, criers, and vendors, and crossed it quickly to the nicer part of town. Barely nicer, but nicer. The food here wouldn't be half rat feces.

Most days, he just stopped at whichever street cart he saw first and bought whatever they had that would make a suitably filling meal. Usually hand pies or kebabs, or all manner of eggs mixed with various combinations of meat and vegetables.

Today, though, he felt he'd earned something a bit nicer. He settled on his favorite bakery, a place he typically only visited for any cheap, stale remains he could get at the end of the day, which normally wasn't much, as other people always got there first.

The scents of bread and sugar and fresh coffee washed over him as he stepped into the shop, the cheerful bell over the door tinkling. The large woman behind the counter, Anya, lifted a hand in greeting, but kept her attention on the customers she was dealing with, one of those who thought the fact they lived just a street over from the slums meant they were suddenly better than all the people they used to live with.

Tashi returned the silent greeting in kind and went over to where Anya's husband was manning the counter where all the pastries, sandwiches, and other such fair was kept for people to pop in and grab a quick meal before returning to their bustling day.

"Hey, Tashi, haven't seen your ugly face for a while," the man, Grigori, said with a smile.

"If I come too often, your wife will realize she could have married up instead of down," Tashi retorted. "Give me whatever you recommend. I need a big breakfast or lunch or whatever time of day it is."

Grigori laughed. "Right between the two, if you go by normal folk hours." He bustled about behind the counter, and in short order handed over a large paper packet. "One'll do there, Tashi, and here's a coffee for you."

Tashi gave him one, took the coffee, and with another wave to Anya, headed back out. He settled in a tiny bit of 'park' that was really just a crowd of benches and standing tables on a sad patch of grass, and unwrapped his food.

As ever, Grigori had given him far more than a single col should have bought. The non-existent debt the couple felt they owed had been long ago repaid, but they insisted on being too nice to him all the time anyway.

All Tashi could do in return was keep praying they'd never need his services a second time.

He removed the bottom portion of his mask so he could eat and set it to hand nearby. Taking a large bite of a flaky pastry stuffed with sausage, egg, peppers and onions, he finally pulled out the notes from his mailbox and looked them over.

The first was predictable, if unpleasant. The asylum at the edge of the slums was always losing patients—sometimes genuinely, more often to abuse or at the request of people who wanted the family embarrassment out of the way. Everyone sympathized with a family forced to mourn a lost loved one. Everyone whispered about the families that produced a crazy.

It was a fate Tashi could have easily found himself enduring, save that there were simply too many ways it could have gone wrong. His mother detested variables.

Of course, thoughts of his mother reminded him she was dying—cursed. Somehow it had become *his* fucking job to save her. Talk about a twisted fate. He hoped she choked on it when she realized who had saved her.

Well, first he had to do the saving.

He shuffled to the second note, which was far less predictable. Someone down Midden needed a body removed. No details, of course, just a meeting point. Interesting, interesting. Usually any bodies that made it down to Midden, also known as Shit Row, were of the 'just bits and pieces' variety. There was never enough left for anyone to care about. On the rare occasion there was, the Midden knew how to take care of their own problems. He'd never known them to need a body catcher.

Finishing the sausage pastry, he moved on to the next in the packet, this one stuffed with nuts and spices and honey. Once upon a time, he'd eaten a much fancier version of these for breakfast nearly every day, alongside a pot of coffee and chocolate that cost more than an entire meal for most people.

He tucked the notes away and contemplated his options as he finished eating, occasionally pausing for sips of the coffee, which was perfect, no obscene price required.

He could head to the asylum and see what

he'd be in for that evening, so he knew what equipment to bring and what cantrips he'd likely use, in case he needed to account for an unusual amount of energy depletion.

Or he could start with going to Midden to see what in the world had happened there that required him.

His last option for how to start his day was to begin with curse hunting, and that meant figuring out where to start, which meant getting a touch closer to his old life than he or anyone else wanted.

Tashi sighed and tucked the last few bits of food away to eat for dinner, sipping at his coffee as he pushed to his feet. Because it wasn't really a hard decision. He hated the asylum, and he would avoid the problem of his family for as long as possible. To Shit Row it was, and may the problem be an easy one, though he doubted it. Midden never needed any outside help. What had changed that?

He was about to find out. At least he had a full belly and good coffee.

Chapter Three

The fastest way to get to Midden was via the Sun—Sunrise Boulevard, though only outsiders called it that. But the Sun was also crowded, *visible*, and even with a mask on, he preferred to avoid places where a lot of people would see him.

So the better route to Midden was to head down Tanner St to Fisher Row and north on to Midden.

He finished his coffee halfway to Tanner and tossed the cup, then restored the bottom portion of his mask. Like most in that part of the city, his mask was cheaply made, little more than chips and scraps that had been pasted together and then treated like normal wood. His was painted in dark blue and dark red stripes, the eyes and lips rimmed thinly in white. Once upon a time, he'd worn masks made of paper-thin gold, or delicate porcelain, or the finest ebony polished to a gleam inside and painted elaborately on the front. He'd had more of them than he could remember, trusting servants to know which he should use at any given part of the day.

When he'd first been thrown out, he hadn't had one at all, which had made it even more difficult to settle in. Masks were ubiquitous in Ossiri. Anyone without one was an outsider, not to be trusted. Once he'd scraped together enough money to buy one, life had gotten much easier. Not easy. But easier.

Now he had three—day, night, and formal, the absolute bare necessity.

Tanner Street, as usual, smelled appalling. This whole portion of the city did, between Lime, Tanner, Fisher, Midden, and more. The whole broad area was called the Rotter, and it didn't help it butted right up against the Bone Yard on the north end and the Old City at the east end.

Reaching the corner of Tanner and Fisher, he headed west until he came to what was roughly the middle of Midden and from there headed ever so slightly northwest, as Midden Row cut diagonally across the city.

One of these days he really needed to splurge on some mint oil that he could coat on the inside of his mask to help ward off the stench of his work. But one bottle of oil was the equivalent of several meals, and Tashi had no intention of ever going hungry again. He'd done that for six months while he struggled to relearn how to live. He'd been damned lucky it was only six months.

He slowed as he drew close to the location, keeping an eye out for the house number he sought. Midden wasn't somewhere he visited often, save in passing, so he wasn't as familiar with it as he was the rest of Eastbridge.

There it was. Number three. He slipped down the almost too-narrow passage between buildings and, following instructions, pulled open the unlocked gate that led to the backyard and slipped inside. The gate clacked shut behind him, the only immediate noise in the small, rundown yard he now stood in. It was more mud and cracked stone than anything, with a clothesline, a washing tub, and a rain barrel occupying most of the space.

A woman knelt on the ground at the tub, furiously scrubbing, red-faced and exhausted looking. She paused as she noticed Tashi. "Whatta you want?"

"I have a note."

"Ah. Inside, then. You'll find him, I imagine."

Tashi did as told. Inside, the house was as clean and tidy as a house in the Midden could be, and even smelled moderately better. The kitchen was empty, but he found another person in the front room, smoking a pipe that smelled truly foul as he stared into a sad excuse for a fire. The man was long, thin, but had some muscle to him.

He also had horns sticking out of his head, though he'd sawed them down to where they could be easily hidden by a cap. Patches of black and red scales were visible across his nose, scattered around his neck and his bare calves, where his feet were soaking in some solution, probably salts and herbs to ease pain. His hair was short, thick, and curly, and the color of fresh blood. He had black, sharply pointed nails, and red-brown eyes with more in common with a snake than a human. He was absolutely stunning, a patch of unexpected beauty in a miserable place.

He was also a feral, the rather rude name given to those races that weren't entirely human (by the arbitrary standards of humans) but weren't beast either, but a variety of combinations that made some love them, many hate them, and too many fetishize them.

The man lifted a brow. "Got a staring problem?" The question was asked idly, levelly, but the eyes said he wouldn't hesitate to beat sense and manners into Tashi if it proved necessary.

"My apologies," Tashi said. "Hadn't expected to see a Wellow feral in the Midden."

"How do you be knowing one feral from another? First that's marked it since I got here, and I been here awhile," the man said. "Name's Vyra.

You the one I left a message for?"

"I am," Tashi said. "Knowing one feral from another ain't hard. No different than knowing one human from another. What's the Midden want with me?"

Vyra grunted and pulled his feet from the water, then bent and retrieved socks and shoes. "I'll show you. Easier than explaining."

Stranger and stranger.

Tashi waited in silence as Vyra laced his boots, shrugged into a threadbare jacket with more patches and holes than fabric, and pulled on a cheap mask painted with red and green swirls. When he was ready, Tashi silently followed him back outside and to the street. From there, they walked quickly to the south end of the Midden, then down an alleyway that nearly had Tashi gagging from the stench.

Few things smelled worse than a rotting body, but the Midden somehow managed to find all those scents and cram them together.

As they came out of the narrow alleyway, a building closer to falling over than to standing loomed ominously. It was made of the same desultory gray stone as everything in Eastbridge, because it was cheap and readily available, unlike the far fancier woods and stonework that were used in Westbridge.

"What is this?" Tashi asked, something about the building grating on his nerves, like being forced to listen to someone chew, loudly and open-mouthed, for hours on end. There was nothing remarkable about it, just one more derelict building, with a sign too faded and worn to read what its purpose had once been. There were signs of rat and other vermin all over, and the lingering stench and feel of death said more than a few people had died here—murdered, drunks who went one bottle too far, wounded thieves hiding from frogs, and more besides. All the usual reasons people died in Eastbridge, especially in the dark and dreary area known as the Rotter.

"Old processing plant, turned refuse into fertilizer that got shipped out too farms and the like. Was shut down when it was discovered there was a bit too much human in the mix," Vyra said. "Come on. I found it last night when I was looking around for anything I could sell."

"It," Tashi echoed. Nope, he did not like that remotely.

Vyra kept walking, avoiding the entrance and leading Tashi to a side door that was barely holding on by one hinge. They stepped over and around debris, Tashi accidentally sending an old, dark green glass bottle skittering into a chunk of fallen wall.

The day was full of sunshine, but you couldn't tell it in that dreary place. He resisted the urge to call up some lights, though. He didn't advertise his magic unless there was no other choice.

Thankfully, as they pushed onward, more light came through a hole where the ceiling and floors above had collapsed. "How long has this place been closed?"

"More than a year, not quite two," Vyra replied. "It was in a bad state when they shut it down—part of the reason they did so. Nobody gives a single damn about Shit Row, but they don't want a large stack of bodies because they were too cheap to build properly either. So they shut it down and moved it to the docks."

The pieces came together in Tashi's head. "Oh, this is where Rhymer & Stork used to be headquartered. Pretty sure they still don't care if human bodies wind up in the mix."

"We always called it Stormer. This way. Watch your step." Vyra led the way down what was barely identifiable as stairs, into a gloomy basement that stank of death and magic. The magic was so strong, and so foul, it felt like insects crawling over every bit of his skin.

When they finally reached what Vyra wanted to show him, Tashi was surprised and not. He removed his mask so he could see the whole mess unimpeded. "Do you know what this is?"

Vyra shook his head and removed his own mask, clipping it to the front of his jacket. "No, only that it's bad *lala*. Pretty clear you do, though. Interesting skill for a body catcher."

"Yes," Tashi said flatly, taking the sight in again, half-hoping he'd imagined the mess. It was still there, though, in full, grisly glory.

Three bodies in the center, spread out like children making fairies in the snow, their heads together. They lay within a circle of blood, surrounded by a long, intricate cantrip written in blood, closed in another circle. Something like this would have taken many hours spread over at least two days, and up to four, depending on the skills and stamina of the mage.

"What is it?" Vyra asked.

"An insanity cantrip, more or less," Tashi replied. "It hasn't been activated yet, but when it is, every last person within a certain radius—and with three bodies that radius is great—will go mad. Given how easily such madness spreads without magic…"

Vyra flinched, and for good reason: in times of chaos, ferals were usually the first to start being harmed and killed. Their only mistake in life had been to be born part fae, but that never stopped anyone. "Why would someone do that?"

"A good question, but I don't have any answers. You did, however, hire the right body catcher for the job. Go now, and don't talk to anyone about this, not even your—uh, wife or sister or whoever she is."

"Sister," Vyra said with a laugh. "Thank you."

"Don't thank me until I fix the problem. Now shoo."

Vyra went, smiling tentatively—and

prettily—before he slipped his mask back on and headed off.

When he was gone, Tashi crouched by the western edge of the circle, resting his forearms on his knees. Safir was dead. His mother was cursed and going to die soon. Now there was a Circle of Blood Frenzy in the heart of the Rotter? What in the Seven and Eternal Night was going on? He rose and walked slowly around the perimeter of the circle, studying the elaborate cantrip, ignoring the growing headache it was giving him.

Finally, as he was on the verge of throwing up from the head-splitting pain, he found what he sought: a mark of binding. Five parts, so there were five more of these in the city. That was a lot of dead people, and enough to drive the whole city insane.

This had to be related to his mother. It was entirely too much coincidence to be something wholly separate. Kill the queen, cause chaos, take over? Simple but effective.

Ugh, none of this should be his problem. He was twelve years disowned, twelve years forgotten, twelve years forsaken by everyone he thought loved him. Why should he be stuck solving their problems?

Still, if the Blood Frenzy was cast, a whole lot of people would die, and in the aftermath, even more people would be punished, executed, even though none of it would be their fault. Nobody would realize a cantrip was responsible until far too late.

He couldn't leave it, but destroying it would likely bring the mage behind it down on him, since the destruction would leave a tell-tale residue that Tashi simply didn't have the power to hide. Skill, yes, but not power. That required all the fancy baubles and trinkets he'd left behind, jewels of power to supplement his natural abilities.

Sighing, Tashi drew his knife and cut open his finger, whispering a cantrip that would keep the tiny wound from closing. Then he set to work writing his own cantrip over the current one. He had to stop to throw up twice, and his head hurt so badly he wanted to cry, but there was no helping it. He couldn't leave such a deadly cantrip, especially since it wasn't on a time cast—it was set to activate when the mage responsible triggered it. Them. Six of these across the city. That was terrifying. He'd throw up as many times as he needed.

When he finally finished, he'd gone through three fingers, the tips ragged and sore and hot to the touch. The cantrip was done though. Curling in on himself, Tashi held out one trembling arm, spoke the activating words, and the cantrip came to life in a burst of dark violet light.

Tashi passed out.

~~*

He woke to the tolling of the city hall clock. It was across the river and well into Westbridge, but old magic enabled it to be heard across the whole of the city. Sitting up, groaning as his head disapproved strongly, he looked around. Where in the Eternal Night was he? A bed that had more in common with granite, not that his own was much better. Ramshackle room that smelled of cheap candles and the constant shit-stain of Midden.

Right. He'd passed out after sealing that gods-forsaken cantrip. How had he gone from there to here? Vyra? That made the most sense. Only one way to find out.

He climbed out of bed, groaning and swearing at his head, and stumbled his way through a doorway that had been reinforced with scavenged wood. Old anger tried to rise up—at himself, at his family, at all the people he'd once known who could help everyone in the slums easily but never would.

Simmering in that anger wouldn't help, though. So he shunted it away again and focused on the here and now, just like everyone else in Eastbridge.

The stairs were even more alarming than the doorway, but Tashi was used to treacherous stairs in falling down buildings. He braced one hand—the fingertips meticulously bandaged with what looked like repurposed cloth, probably an old shirt or skirt—on the wall and moved slowly and carefully.

Downstairs, he could hear someone moving around in the kitchen, or at least where he remembered the kitchen being, if he was where he thought.

Thankfully, he proved correct: Vyra was puttering around in the kitchen, putting together a meal that smelled like fish. The fishmongers were always willing to sell their leftover goods for dirt cheap after sunset, though only to their fellow Rotters, so it was a frequent meal amongst the poor.

"How did I get here?" Tashi asked.

Vyra turned and set a couple of bowls of thin fish soup on the table. "I hung around after you told me to leave. Saw some strange light. When you didn't emerge after a while, I went to see if you were all right. Which you were not. Bleeding everywhere, damn near the color of fresh snow. You're a bit more than you appear, body catcher. Sit and eat before you fall down."

"Thank you," Tashi said, too tired and sore and hungry to argue. He dropped into the nearest seat and went to work on the soup, not even bothering with the spoon, just drinking it down.

Chuckling, Vyra ate his own soup more sedately. "Mages."

Tashi set his bowl down with a heavy thunk. "You seal a high-level curse with no supplementary power whatsoever and not be ravenous when you're done."

"I'm smart enough to leave that foolishness to crazy mages. They're gonna be after you."

"I know, but they won't come looking as quickly as they would if I'd simply broken it," Tashi said, sad his soup was gone, but he'd never be so rude as to ask for more. You were lucky to get firsts in the Rotter, let alone seconds. "Thank you for saving me and feeding me."

Vyra cast him a wry look. "You just saved me and all the rest of the Midden from a really nasty cantrip. I think the least I can do is drag your sorry ass into bed and give you some bland fish soup."

Tashi smiled in gratitude. "That's not how the Rotter be, and you know it, so thank you. What's a fae like you doing in the Midden?"

"What's a ponce doing in the Rotter?"

"Same thing as everyone else: living with my mistakes and just trying to keep in food and a roof."

"Fair enough." Vyra finished his soup and rose smoothly. He set his dishes in a battered tub to be washed at a public fountain later and took the pot off the beat-up old woodstove that was all the warmth the house probably got. He dumped the remaining contents into Tashi's bowl. "Eat up, mage."

"What about your sister?"

"She would rather go back into the asylum our parents once threw her in than eat fish, mostly because fish was all she ever ate in that place."

"The one by the boneyard?"

"The very same."

Tashi made a face. "I'm glad she's out. I get a lot of work from that place. Which reminds me, I'm supposed to be going there tonight, in fact. I need to get moving."

"What do I owe you?"

"Nothing," Tashi said, and held up a hand when Vyra started to protest. "You saved me, you fed me. Keep my magic between us and we're level."

Vyra huffed. "Fine. Sure you don't want to stay and rest up a bit more?"

"I would love to, but I don't refuse paying work, and my reputation can't take just not showing up to a job."

"You can barely stand."

Tashi shrugged. "Doesn't matter."

Vyra eyed him pensively, then said slowly, "Well… what about some help? I was just let go, got nothing to do with my nights right now. I could help you for the night."

The idea was tempting. More tempting than Tashi liked admitting. He always worked alone. Never again was he going to be stupid enough to trust someone to help him, to have his back.

But his head hurt, and he was exhausted, and even after he finished at the asylum, he would still have to get to work on the curse plaguing his mother. Would it kill him to accept help just once? There were worse fates than having a handsome, sexy, soft-spoken assistant for an evening.

"Fine," he said. "I admit help would be nice tonight. I can't pay much, but I'll do the best I can."

"I thought I was helping you to pay for the work you did *here*. You're a stubborn ass, body catcher."

"It's Tashi, by the way, and yes, I've heard that complaint before." Most often from his worthless mother.

"Tashi," Vyra replied with a soft, pretty smile. "Pleasure to meet you."

"Honor is mine," Tashi replied. "Shall we get to work?"

"Let me grab a few things." Vyra headed up the rickety stairs and returned after a couple of minutes wearing a threadbare black jacket with patches at the elbow, one shoulder, and the pockets, and a lumpy knitted black cap that he pulled down low to cover his head thoroughly and shade his eyes slightly. "All set, boss." He winked.

Tashi refused to note anything about that. He was being stupid enough, and likely it was just an effect of his recent interaction with Rumér. Shaking it off, he said, "Let's go, then," and led the way out into the shit-ridden night.

Chapter Four

Thankfully, being in the Midden put them significantly closer to their destination that he would have been starting at his flat.

All the way to the northeast of the city, at the edge of the slums and butting up against the Old City, was what locals called the boneyard. Once it had been a knackery, and much like the old factory where Tashi had just sealed a cantrip, had been the source of gossip and rumors about them processing humans alongside all the animals that were dragged there. Probably not true, as knackers were watched pretty closely for such things—it was far more likely problems would come from the farmers and such who paid the knackers—but it made for good gossip over a cup of shitty beer.

Unfortunately, not long after Tashi had found himself on the streets relearning how to live, the knackery had burned to the ground. Nothing left but ruins and bones, the knackery had been rebuilt elsewhere, and no one had purchased the land to be repurposed. Odd, because the land would be valuable, even if it was at the ass end of the slums, but that wasn't Tashi's problem. As long as it remained abandoned, he had one more place to stash the bodies he caught.

Right next to the boneyard was the asylum, officially called the Goldbird Lunatic Asylum. Near as Tashi had ever been able to tell, it contained about ten percent genuinely insane people, fifteen percent people who should be in prison or dead, and seventy-five percent people who'd been put well out of the way by family, friends, or someone else in whom they'd misplaced their trust. It was one of the most depressing places in the city.

He bypassed the front entirely and looped around the back, crossing the yard to the door intended for receiving deliveries of food, medicine, and so forth. He rapped on the door three times, then another two after a pause.

A moment later the small vision panel in the top portion of the door slid open with a rusty creak and familiar gray eyes scowled out at him. "Took you long enough. Was about to have Ezhil come back, take these too."

Ezhil had been here? What a shame they hadn't crossed paths so Tashi could punch his stupid face. "Busy night. You wanna let me in or do it yourself?"

Grumbling, the woman slammed the panel shut, and then came the sound of the six locks that kept the door secured, as there were understandably a great many creative, determined patients who wanted out. "Who the fuck is that?"

"My assistant, and it's a good thing, since it sounds like you got more than one tonight. Stop your bitching, he's Midden."

The woman grunted and slammed the door shut, setting all the locks back in place. "Fine, whatever. Come this way. One funny move, though, and I'll have to send for Ezhil to take care of you."

"You send for Ezhil to take care of my body, I will crawl out of wherever he puts me and eat you in your sleep, Oshtka. Understand me?"

She snorted and shoved open a heavy set of doors, leading further into the depths of the building. "Like anything you can say would scare me after all I see and hear around this place. Save your threats for people who think death sounds like a bad idea."

Tashi couldn't really argue with that, so he just sighed and then fell silent. Vyra gave him a look that was equal parts amusement and curiosity, but Tashi just shook his head slightly, signaling he'd answer questions later.

The hall they were in was dark, the mage lights set there flickering and wavering, in sore need of renewing. As always, the place reeked of mold, mildew, and things he preferred not to think about. This hall was theoretically filled with surgeries and offices, but Tashi would bet a month's rent that no real doctor had ever set foot in the place, except maybe to stand at the reception desk to hastily sign a stack of death certificates that someone else had helpfully filled out for him. Half had ordinary doors with glass panels in the top half, though all the glass was dusty, broken, and covered in all manner of grime, including the odd bloody handprint.

The remaining doors were all the swinging kind found in surgeries, kitchens, and the sort, that could swing out either way and would easily crack open the head of the unwise or inexperienced. Oshtka walked to the end of the hall, to the last of the swinging door, and strode briskly through it.

Lying on body slabs were three corpses, just visible in the weak light of an old, smokey oil lamp. Tashi whispered a cantrip to summon light of his own, soft and bluish, and set it to hang in the middle of the ceiling, giving him a clear view of the bodies.

All three had died of suicide, their wrists deeply, severely cut in the same way: a straight line from the base of the palm to halfway down the forearm, and then a horizontal cut right across the wrist. How in the world had they each managed to do that to themselves once, let alone a second time? "What in the Eternal Night happened here?"

"Natural causes," Oshtka replied curtly. "Take care of it. You'll get your pay like always."

Tashi didn't bother to reply as she left, the door swinging behind her before coming slowly to a standstill. Just pinched the bridge of his nose and breathed in, out, until he felt moderately less murderous.

Vyra approached the nearest of the three bodies, gently touching the woman's cheek. "This is horrible. Who did this to them? There's no way they could have done it to themselves."

"You'd be surprised what people do to themselves and each other when suitably motivated or out of their goddess-damned minds. That being said, I agree with you. This looks like ritual work, though what ritual they were tricked into, I couldn't say." He chanted a cantrip and snapped his fingers, and a rainbow of sparks ran across the body he was in front of. One by one the multitude of colors died, until they were left with only the oil lamp and mage light above. "Nothing magic involved. Probably one of the other patients convinced them of something or drugged them and did something. Night, the staff could have done this if suitably paid by the people who had these poor bastards locked up. Sadly, too many possibilities. I doubt we'll ever know the truth. That's how it usually goes around here."

"I knew it was bad, just on what little I saw when I came to rescue my sister, but fuck. Your job is even more depressing than I imagined, though I'll be honest and say I never thought about it until I suddenly needed your services." He hesitated, then shook his head slightly, and asked, "So what do we do now?"

"Now we take them to the boneyard, and after that, we go visit one of my stashes," Tashi said. "Hope you like digging holes."

"Can't be worse than shoveling shit," Vyra said with a sigh. "How do you expect to carry three bodies between us? One is more than enough work for two people."

Tashi laughed. "Magic, my dear. Magic." He chanted the cantrips, snapping his finger over each body in turn, leaving them levitating the barest bit. "Now we just push." He nudged one off the table and laughed again at the look of abject horror on Vyra's face. "Surely you've seen this kind of magic before."

"Yes, for moving crates and heavy platters of food and the like. Not a body!" He made an X over his chest and muttered something, likely a prayer. "Never again will I complain about shoveling shit."

"Frankly, I prefer the bodies. Guess it's a good thing our jobs aren't reversed. You can leave if this is too much for you," Tashi said, refusing to feel disappointed at the idea. He worked alone; it was better that way. He wasn't going to start enjoying having a partner. It was just one night. There was nothing to like or get attached to unless you were a complete fool, and he liked to think he was only *mostly* a fool.

"Too much? No. Too much was seeing the state of my sister when I came here to get her. So thin her ribs showed, her hair had been shorn, she could barely talk, and it took roughly an hour of me holding her hand and saying her name and just… rambling… before she stirred enough from wherever she'd gone in her head to keep herself sane to recognize me. Nothing was worse than the way she screamed and sobbed then. I carried her right out of here that very moment, and thankfully none of them were stupid enough to challenge me."

"I would imagine not," Tashi said. "I'm glad you were there for her."

"Wish I'd gotten here sooner," Vyra replied gruffly.

Tashi smiled sourly. "Better late than never, trust me. Now come on, pick a floating body and let's go. I'll handle the other two; I've gotten pretty good at it."

Chuckling softly, shaking his head, Vyra did as told, taking the body of one of the two women, leaving the remaining woman and man for Tashi.

Leading the way, Tashi headed back the

way they'd come, but continued on past the heavily-locked door to the loading doors beside it, which Oshtka had already left unlocked for him. Pushing one of the large, heavy doors open, he guided the bodies outside, then closed the door behind him. By the time they were across the yard, it would be locked again.

The cantrip wasn't the type to last long, so he had to renew it a few times as they walked across the asylum yard, through a disguised gap in the looming fence, and through to the boneyard. He pressed on once they reached it, meticulously searching for the ideal spot to bury them.

He settled for the base of what had once been an enormous furnace, likely to fuel the many tubs in which horses and other animals had been rendered into all manner of household items, from fat and soap all the way to pet food.

Setting the bodies down, he yawned and then said, "All right. Did you want to rest up here or come with me to the stash?"

"I'm not sitting around with three bodies in the boneyard. Call me superstitious, but that's bad *lala*."

"You get used to it. Come on, it's not far." He headed off to the back end of the boneyard, where it started to blend into the Old City, and continued onward, until they reached the crumbling remains of what had once been someone's house. In the middle of the front room, he used magic and some judicious shoving to move some heavy rocks, revealing a trap door. Opening it, he climbed down the rickety steps and, with Vyra's help, hauled up bags of lime and lye, as well as a couple of shovels, since he always kept spares, should one break or rust or have to be abandoned.

After they had enough, and he'd rehidden the stash entrance, a quick cantrip and they were headed back to the waiting bodies.

That, of course, was when the fun work began. "This is why I prefer the river," he said as he set to shoveling. "Riskier to get the bodies to the river, but man is disposing of them easier once you're there."

Vyra laughed and shook his head. "What strange problems you have."

"Surely the Midden has its own peculiar problems."

"Aye, and that includes remains," Vyra replied. "More often just, uh, bits and pieces, though, rarely the entire body. Little stuff, mostly, like fingers, toes, sometimes a whole hand or foot, even more rarely a whole limb. But it's nothing nefarious the way people like to go on about. People lose them in accidents, surgeries… and just throw them out. Friend of mine found a head once working the hospitals one night. Glad I wasn't on that shift."

"I wish I only had to deal with parts. Be a sight easier than moving entire bodies, and I even have an advantage most body catchers don't."

Vyra glanced at him, clearly curious about his magic, but thankfully said nothing. Tashi would have told him to shove off, and he really didn't want to be rude to such a surprisingly amiable companion.

It took them what felt like ages to dig the three holes, working only by moonlight and a small mage light that Tashi kept muted and close to the ground. By the time they were done, he was filthy, sweaty, and ready to crawl into one of the graves himself just for a nice, cool nap. Instead, he thunked the blade of his shovel into the ground and cast cantrips for lightness, canceling each one as they rolled the bodies into their respective graves. After that came the lime and lye, followed by filling in the holes.

By the time they finished *that*, hazy gray morning light was beginning to tease along the edges of the world. "Come on, we'll get our pay, I'll buy you breakfast, and I guess that's that."

"That's that," Vyra echoed, oddly subdued—though he must have been at least as exhausted as Tashi, so maybe not all that odd in the end. "How do you do this night after night? I thought shoveling shit was exhausting, but this is something else entirely."

"Why do you think I prefer the river?" Tashi asked with a laugh as they headed back to the asylum.

As always, his money was waiting for him

in an empty can set amongst garbage that would be hauled away later that day. He gave half to Vyra, waving away his attempts to protest. "Come on, let's get cleaned up and find some food."

Out on the street, though, they hadn't gone more than a couple of blocks when he heard shouting—city guards and a familiar, much despised voice full of unexpected panic. Hurrying to the intersection, he pressed up against the corner of a building and peered around.

Sure enough, Ezhil was being harassed by guards, his face and clothes bloody from a broken nose, and from the way he held his arm, they'd roughed him up thoroughly. Why? Ezhil was an annoying, obnoxious, disrespectful piece of shit, but like anyone in the body business, he didn't tend to draw attention where he could avoid it. Especially from the fucking frogs. What especially stupid, cocky thing had he done to put himself in their line of sight? How much did Tashi really care? If Ezhil was in jail, that was one less problem for him to deal with.

"Who's that?" Vyra asked as the guards mocked and taunted Ezhil, who was clearly wavering on his feet and wouldn't fare well if they went for another round of beatings. "Should we help?"

"Ezhil is his name, and he's… competition, you could say, though he doesn't deserve that much respect."

"Another body catcher?"

"No, he's a body *snatcher*," Tashi replied, lips curling. He didn't just take the bodies and bury them and have done, he took them—or stole them—and sold them off to mages, healers, and anyone else willing to pay his price. It was crass and disrespectful. "Whatever he did, he probably deserves it, the no-good bastard."

Vyra gave him a look. "Is there really that much difference body catchers and snatchers?"

"Is this really the time?"

"So what should we do?"

"Not get involved in something that's going to make my life a thousand times more difficult when I already have enough on my chest?" Tashi replied hopefully.

So far as he was concerned, Ezhil could suffer. The guards probably wouldn't kill him, just arrest him and let him stew for a few days. It happened to all of them. He'd be right back to stealing bodies in a couple of weeks, a month at most.

On the other hand, Ezhil wasn't the kind of person to get beat up by guards. Leaving aside he was a body snatcher and so attention equaled bad, Ezhil simply preferred to keep to himself, or at least it had always seemed to Tashi. Granted, he went out of his way to avoid anything to do with Ezhil, but it was hard not to notice that he was surprisingly quiet for such an obnoxious, annoying asshole.

"I'm going to regret this," he muttered. "I'll

distract the guards; you get Ezhil out of there. Meet up at the Rose."

"Got it."

Chapter Five

Stifling a groan oven his own gross stupidity, Tashi called up his magic, closing his eyes as he focused on the cantrips he needed. When he had them, he opened his eyes and cast them, drawing them quickly and deftly, jerking his head as he threw them out into the street.

There was an explosion of light and noise, causing the guards to jerk and recoil, shift their focus from Ezhil.

Tashi cast the next set of cantrips—more light, more noise, but also illusions of shadows, movement, as though there was a crowd of people moving toward them. The confused, panicked guards drew their weapons, and Ezhil more or less ceased to exist.

He waited until Vyra had Ezhil, then cast one more light show for good measure before bolting off in the other direction, not running, as that would draw attention, but not taking his merry old time about it either.

He made his way south, taking a meandering route, but not so strange that he'd draw the attention of anyone out and about. Not that anyone around here was likely to ask or answer questions. Guards knew better than to try—or to come with a damned good bribe.

Once he was far enough away from the mess nobody would even think to associate it with him, he paused at a cart for some strong black tea, paying extra for cream and sugar, and gulped it down as he continued walking.

He passed through perfume district, slang for the portion of the Rotter where most of the brothels were located. All cheap and suspicious on this side of the river, the kind that robbed you while you slept instead of just charging the fortune upfront, but nobody complained much when there was an itch they needed scratching and somebody else would just steal the money anyway.

Of those brothels, there were only a couple that Tashi visited, and not frequently. When he had to conduct business, or something similar, though, he opted for the Rose. Its full name was the House of the Rose in Bloom, which was a fancy way of saying House of the Excited Cunt.

Not a very popular brothel, which meant they were happy to take whatever money they could get, making them ideal as a meeting spot.

By the time he reached it, faint hints of morning were turning the sky a dingy gray, and the growing clouds promised it was going to be a wet and dreary day. Hopefully he'd sleep through the worst of it. Assuming he *got* to sleep, which seemed to be an increasing challenge lately. He didn't like that one little bit. Hopefully all this extra work would make up for the slower times later.

Finishing his tea, he tossed the paper cup it had come in and hastened the last block to the Rose. Climbing the stairs, he rapped on the door. When the viewing slot opened, he said, "Let me in, Karli."

"Hey, Tashi," Karli replied, and slid the opening closed before swinging the door open wide. Closing it, he grinned and said, "Your friends are already upstairs."

"A curse on you for calling that reprobate body snatcher my friend," Tashi retorted, flipping Karli a coin. "We're not here."

"Obviously. Usual room."

Lifting a hand in thanks, Tashi pressed onward, climbing rickety stairs covered in questionable stains, the wallpaper peeling to reveal walls with even more alarming stains. He could only imagine what might turn up if the walls were ever knocked down. Thankfully, not his problem. He mostly dealt with fresher matters.

Up and up he went, to the third floor that was really just a converted attic, with holes and mildew and everything else that came with a poorly maintained house. He rapped on the door and then opened it, and sighed in relief to see Vyra there, sitting at a table sipping at what looked much like the tea Tashi had bought. "You made it, good."

"That was quite the distraction," Vyra said with a laugh. "I think even your friend here was impressed."

"If one more person calls that bone-banger my friend—"

"Don't worry," Ezhil said, his voice as infuriatingly beautiful as ever, deep and warm, nothing at all like the cretin it belonged to. "I'm not enjoying it either. The day I call some smarmy, self-righteous body catcher a friend is the day I decide to become a priest."

"They wouldn't let you in the temple." Tashi stepped further into the room, kicked the door shut, and leaned against it with his arms folded across his chest. "What did you do to finally get the ass kicking you deserve?"

Ezhil rolled his eyes. Which were a pale, delicate blue, like fine china or the most delicate crystal. The man was ridiculously beautiful, from the top of his dark-flame hair to the tips of his grimy but costly boots, with pale brown skin, freckles, and a mouth that would be pretty if every word he said wasn't massively irritating. "Why do you care? For that matter, why did you stick your fingers in it? Had nothing to do with you, catcher."

"You're clear of trouble, does the why of it really matter?"

"I want to know just how badly this sudden display of kindness is going to nip me in the balls later."

"Your balls are too small for anyone to bother nipping," Tashi replied. "Seriously, what did you do to piss off the guards, and how is it going to make life more miserable for the rest of us?"

Ezhil gave him a pensive look that Tashi didn't like *remotely*. "Funny you of all people should ask and be the one to help me. Those guards were scouring the Rotter for a body snatcher who uses illegal magic. Those maggots never could be bothered to sort out the difference between snatchers and whiny body catchers."

Ice ran down Tashi's spine. "What in the Eternal Night are you talking about? Why would they be looking for a snatcher or catcher with illegal magic?"

"I didn't ask them, Your Highness," Ezhil replied, rolling his eyes. Tashi *really* hated when Ezhil called him that, even though the dumbass had no idea just how accurate he was being. "I told them to piss off like usual, and when that didn't work, I encouraged them to do so with more colorful language. They didn't take too kindly to that. Then out of nowhere, there's a fancy light show and here you are: a body catcher using magic you probably ain't licensed to. I'd heard rumors you used magic in your trade, Tashi, but I always thought it was just gin-induced nonsense."

"Your face is nonsense," Tashi retorted reflexively. Fuck. Fuck fuck fuck. Why would frogs be looking for him? Maybe it was somebody else? That was unlikely, though. He only knew of a couple of others in the body business who used magic, and they used what amounted to street flash, just enough to garner attention and coin, but no real substance to it. None of them could hold a candle to him.

None of them were royal princes trained up to serve the next queen as Warlock Prime. Fuck. Who was looking for him so loudly? They were going to get him killed, or worse, ruin his reputation and livelihood!

This reeked of his sister, as domineering and ruthless as their mother. Which meant this probably related to his mother. Which in turn meant that as per usual, nobody in the palace was communicating with each other.

Still, things must be worse with his mother than he'd already thought if his sister was desperate enough to try and find him. She'd just have to keep trying. He wasn't going to be dragged back by the people who threw him out just because he was suddenly useful again. Fuck them.

"I'll take care of it," he said when Ezhil kept staring at him expectantly.

"You'd better," Ezhil said, "because after your stupid stunt—"

"The stupid stunt where I saved you from jail at the very least and your life at most?"

"*Your stupid stunt* they're going to think that I at least know who they're looking for—and they're not wrong, and it's not like I'd lose sleep getting you out of my way once and for all."

"Kindness is more expensive than selfish," Tashi muttered. It was a well-worn saying in the Rotter, and he'd yet to see it prove untrue. "Do whatever in Eternal Night makes you happy, you lazy, ungrateful ass crust. I'm out of here. Vyra, come on, we'll get that promised breakfast." He stormed out of the room and back down the ominously creaking stairs, out onto the street, where he took several gulps that didn't reek of moldy sweat and crusty spunk.

Footsteps sounded behind him, and Tashi turned to apologize for his abrupt departure—and stopped when he saw Vyra wasn't alone. "Aren't I done with you, snatcher?"

"Oh, shut up, and let's go get breakfast," Ezhil said. "Then I can wash my hands of you and get back to doing real work."

"Fucking your sister isn't real work, not to hear her tell it."

Ezhil laughed. "I hate you, Tashi. What do

you want to eat?"

Vyra replied, "Don't really come this far out of the Midden, not since I managed to get my sister out of that nightmare asylum."

Ezhil gave him a look of genuine horror. "Your *sister* was in that place? Did she at least murder enough people to deserve it?"

"How many murders is enough to justify being sent to Goldbird?" Tashi asked dryly. "Because I feel some of the staff qualify for admittance."

Ezhil snorted a laugh. "Shut up, don't make me laugh at your stupid comments. It goes against everything I believe in. You're not wrong, though. Alright, Midden, if you've never been this side of the Rotter before, we have to go to the Saucy Grill. Griddle cakes like you wouldn't believe and coffee that actually tastes like coffee, not something scooped out of the toilet and boiled until burned. But this is the last fucking time I do anything remotely nice for you, Your Highness."

"What would it take for you to stop calling me that?"

"You don't make enough money, even when you steal it off the bodies you catch."

Vyra rolled his eyes. "You two bicker like an old married couple. My parents sounded exactly the same growing up. Griddle cakes and coffee sound wonderful."

"This way, then," Ezhil said, motioning for them to follow, like Tashi didn't know exactly where they were going.

When he'd first been thrown out, he'd known nothing about the Rotter. He'd been robbed, beaten, and cheated as he learned his way around, and now he knew it like he'd lived there his whole life. If Ezhil kept treating him like a lack-brain, he was going to find himself lacking a head before the sun was fully up.

Thankfully, Ezhil subsided into silence the rest of the trip. Tashi was more than happy to do the same, breaking it with nothing more than the occasional yawn. What he wouldn't give for a chance to sleep for several hours without interruption. The luxury of the wealthy, just one of many true luxuries he'd never appreciated until he didn't have it anymore. He'd take sound sleep over gold any day, but it took gold to gain the life that afforded sound sleep.

There really was no winning in the Rotter.

The Saucy Grill—just called the Sauce by locals—was already bustling when they arrived, but Ezhil must have a connection because somehow a table was available for them right by one of the street-facing windows.

A woman with curly gray hair and two straight, spiraling horns coming out of the top of her head bustled up to their table, setting down cups and a pot of coffee before tousling Ezhil's hair. "Didn't think I'd see you for hours yet, love." She quirked a brow at Tashi, then smiled at Vyra like he was her long-lost son, switching to

Contiga, a pidgin used by ferals, based primarily on Tigia, but with significant supplements from other languages.

Tashi knew Tigia, but he was still shit at Contiga. The coffee was vastly more interesting than trying to eavesdrop on a conversation anyway. He gulped his first cup down, heedless of the way it burned the roof of his mouth, then poured a second one. "What did you do or not do that she calls you 'love'? Does someone pay her?"

"She's my *aunt*, you puss-riddled dick."

"Think about my dick a lot, do you?"

"You wi—"

"Oh, knock it off," the woman said. "Honestly, Ezi, are you twelve? You want your usual, I take it. What about you two?"

"House plate," Tashi said. "Vyra here has never had the pleasure, so ruin him for anywhere else."

Vyra laughed. "The coffee already did that."

Smiling, the woman said, "You'll all be taken care of. I'll bring more coffee." She bustled off and vanished quickly in the chaos of the restaurant, leaving the three of them in silence.

After a couple of minutes, Vyra said, "So what exactly is the animosity between snatcher and catchers?"

"Catchers are paid to take bodies away and dispose of them as respectfully as possible," Tashi said. "Because they're *people*, even the nastiest asshole in existence, and shouldn't be treated like chattel."

Ezhil snorted. "They're corpses. Everything that made the body a person is long gone; who cares what happens to the meat and bones left behind? Much more useful given to scientists and mages and so forth than being dumped in the river or buried in the ground."

"Right, and how would you feel if tomorrow you found out your aunt had been turned into a book binding and dice and preserves in jars for necromantic workings?"

"Nice try, but she already told me she doesn't want to be given to the worms for food; she'd rather be useful. That job is already mine."

Tashi rolled his eyes. "Fair enough, but you have her permission. How often do you bother to get permission for the bodies you sent off to be boiled and strung up for display in some lecture hall?"

"More often than you might think, and what are the others going to do about it? They're dead, Tashi, they don't need their bone sacks anymore."

"Whatever," Tashi muttered bitterly. "People deserve to rest in peace, not be turned into market goods."

Vyra smiled wryly. "Our bodies are commodities while we're alive. Makes sense the trend doesn't change when we're dead. I shovel the shit that becomes fertilizer; eventually I'll be the fertilizer. Just how it goes."

Tashi groaned. "Don't take his side!"

Ezhil laughed.

"I'm not taking any 'side', just saying I see his point. That being said, my sister would be distraught if her body was treated so after she died. I could never let that happen to her. She's been used enough in life, nearly to the point of breaking. She'd want to rest in peace."

"Ugh, you're being reasonable and fair, that's even worse," Tashi replied.

Vyra laughed. "You're too charming to be a body catcher, so why are you doing it?"

"Because some mistakes you can't take back or fix," Tashi replied. "I'm just another sob story in the Rotter, and not even an interesting one."

Ezhil snorted a laugh as he refilled his coffee, eyes flicking up briefly to meet Tashi's. "Whatever you say, Your Highness."

For some reason, the words sent a chill down Tashi's spine this time. Stupid. He just needed sleep. There was no reason for anyone to think him anything more than just another face in the Rotter. A body catcher slightly better than most. At worst, they probably thought he was some poor, fallen noble.

Shaking it off, he gestured crudely at Ezhil for good measure and let his eyes flick around the restaurant for a distraction. The sound of the bell over the door reflexively drew his attention—and the coffee soured in his stomach as he saw two frogs step inside, their notable green uniforms standing out sharply. They looked messy, disheveled, like they'd recently been in a fight that hadn't gone well for them.

Like they'd gotten mixed up in light and noise and illusions.

"Damn it," he said. "Looks like we've been found somehow."

"I'd be willing to bet the Rose had something to do with it," Ezhil said sourly. "Those dung heaps will sell anything and everything." He glanced briefly over his shoulder, then jerked back around. "What should we do?"

"Well, I'm not in the mood for going to jail, so either we try to sneak out, or we cause a distraction and run again."

Vyra shook his head. "Here I though life in the Midden got too brisk for me sometimes."

"Normally everything is incredibly boring," Tashi replied with a sigh. "So what's it going to be?"

"Sneak out," Ezhil said. "The distraction worked once, but I don't trust it to work twice."

"I'm offended you think I only have one trick up my sleeve, but fine," Tashi replied. "Give me your hand then."

"Not a fucking chance. I don't need you and your stupid fucking cantrips to sneak out of a place, Your Highness."

"Stop calling me that," Tashi hissed. "Those

bruises on your face say you need all the help you can get, so swallow your pride, you cocksucking dung heap and give me your hand."

Ezhil slowly held out his hand and with a purr in his voice, said, "Such a sweet talker, Your Highness."

"I hate you with every fiber of my being."

Chapter Six

Tashi cupped the back of Ezhil's hand and traced a sigil into his palm. "You next." Vyra offered his hand over, and Tashi drew the same symbol. "All right. One at a time, get up and leave. Don't hurry or anything, leave just like you would on any ordinary day."

"I'll do my best," Ezhil said, "but an ordinary day for me is saying goodbye to my relatives."

"They'll have to stew in their anguish until they see you next time," Tashi said. "Stop being so fucking annoying and *go* before I give them you as a distraction so I can escape."

Ezhil laughed and rose. "As my prince commands."

Tashi sighed, but said nothing, because the more he responded to Ezhil's stupid comments, the longer it would take him to leave.

When he finally rose and strode off, threading through the crowd with ease, Vyra smiled. "You two are hilarious. Childish, but hilarious."

Oh, good, the cute feral thought he was childish. This day got better and better. "Your turn," he muttered.

"See you outside." Vyra rose and slipped away.

As the guards started to turn away from the bar where they'd been speaking to what looked like the proprietor, Tashi cast the cantrip that faded him from view. Figured the only way to get away from the people looking for him was to use illegal magic that should get him caught even faster.

Maybe his bitch mother should have reconsidered disowning and discarding such a powerful mage. At the very least, she should have sealed off his power, but she probably hadn't wanted to waste that much time. Or had thought he'd die before it became an issue. Her loss. His gain.

He slipped away even as the guards headed for the recently vacated table. Outside, he quickly spied the other two tucked into an alleyway. "See how much easier it is to do literally anything when you keep your mouth shut?"

Tashi realized his mistake the moment Ezhil's stupid smirk appeared. "Some of my talents require I open very, very wide."

"I doubt it," Tashi retorted. "Come on, let's keep moving. We need to find somewhere to lay low."

"My place," Vyra said. "I doubt anyone involved in this mess knows anything about me. I'm not even obviously a feral at a glance. No one is going to hunt for you in the Midden. Come on."

Tashi smiled. "I owe you, Vyra."

"We'll sort it out," Vyra said with an answering smile.

Ezhil rolled his eyes, but for once kept his stupid mouth shut, and the three of them wended their way through the streets back to the Midden.

By the time they arrived, all Tashi wanted to do was fall over. "I need sleep." Then he needed to figure out how to check his mail without getting caught.

"We don't have much, but I'll bring down what spare blankets we do have. My sister likely won't be back until tonight. She won't ask questions." Vyra headed upstairs, steps fading off, and Tashi went to make a fire.

Ezhil dropped into one of the rickety chairs nearby. "So why are they suddenly hunting for you now, Your Highness?"

"Stop calling me that!" Tashi snarled. "It's stupid and annoying and—"

"True." Ezhil stared at him. "Isn't it?"

"Just shut the fuck up." Tashi stabbed viciously at the fire, willing it to cooperate. The silence was oppressive, but he'd be damned if he asked all the questions burning on his tongue.

When the fire was finally going strong, he sat in the other chair to work on his boots, setting them aside once he had them off and folding his outer wear neatly and setting it atop the boots. He then pulled his hair down and combed it out as best he could with his fingers before braiding it up again.

What he wouldn't give for a proper bath, proper meal, proper sleep. Fuck, he'd settle for the sleep.

Vyra returned with the blankets and a single lumpy pillow that had seen better days. "Here's all I could find in the linen cupboard, and my sister's pillow. She won't mind if someone borrows it. Wish I could do better—"

"You're keeping me safe from the frogs, and this after you helped me before," Tashi cut in. "Thank you, Vyra. For everything."

Vyra shrugged the words off, but looked pleased all the same. "Let me know if you need anything further. One we're all awake again, we'll work out a plan, or maybe the guards will have finally given up by then."

"Not likely," Ezhil said. "Not likely at all."

"How many times do I have to tell you to shut up?"

Ezhil smirked, that taunting purr returning

to his voice as he replied, "Sweet prince, if my parents and my ex-wife couldn't get me to shut up, what makes you think you can?"

"I have the magic, little boy. I can literally deprive you of the ability to speak."

Vyra cast him a look. "Isn't that kind of magic illegal?"

"So is everything I do, technically, since I don't have a license. I'm a body catcher. Do you think one stupid cantrip to shut up the world's most annoying body snatcher is going to lose me sleep?"

"You two," Vyra said. "I'm going to bed. Keep the feuding down." He cast Tashi a brief smile and then slipped up the stairs.

Ezhil cast him a look. "You're not going to follow him up there?"

"What? No. Why in the world would I?" He took the pillow and two of the blankets and arranged them on the floor near the fire, reluctantly leaving room for Ezhil.

"That was definitely a 'come ride my cock' smile if ever I saw one."

"You need to stop going to the paint factory to inhale the fumes," Tashi replied. "Go the fuck to sleep, or I'll put you to sleep." So saying, he lay down, got as comfortable as he could sleeping on an uneven, creaky floor, and closed his eyes.

"Yes, Your Highness."

Tashi pinched his mouth shut, refusing to get involved in further bickering, and focused only on going to sleep.

He woke sometime later—long enough the fire was nearly out, and he sorely needed to piss. He threw some new logs on the fire and then hustled outside to attend to business. He was just about to head back inside when he heard commotion on the street. It was late morning, though, if he was guessing correctly. Commotion in the Midden at that time of the day wasn't exactly unusual. Probably someone had fallen in a vat of shit again.

Then he heard a pounding knock on a house nearby, and the ringing tones of a well-trained royal guard bark out, "Open in the name of the Queen!"

Well, fuck. So much for nobody would find him in the Midden. Time to go. Running running running. Always running. Would be nice to have the kind of life where he wasn't always trying to get away from it.

He really should have thought about that sooner. Like say, before committing murder. Oh, well.

Tashi hurried inside, yanked on his boots, jacket, hat, and mask, and then fled out the back door again. Vyra and Fuckhead would be all right if he wasn't there anymore.

He headed to the back fence, taking it at a run, and climbed up and over, landing in a backyard that had more in common with a swamp. Tashi absolutely did not want to know why or how it had gotten that way.

Clearly the situation with his mother was even more dire than he'd thought if his sister of all people was trying to find him. The only way he was going to get any peace was if he got this stupid assignment over with.

Fine, so be it. Time to figure out who was cursing his mother and how. If for no other reason than to prevent those damned Blood Frenzy cantrips from coming to pass. Yet another problem on his pile. Fuck, he was so tired.

All right, focus. A curse that passed for illness and could be cast and maintained from significant distance limited the options significantly. Whoever it was had access, directly or indirectly, to his mother's blood. She was too old for the easiest way to obtain blood from most women, but accidents happened all the time. Even a simple papercut would be sufficient.

First and foremost, the curse would need to be somewhere easily overlooked, a place that did not see a lot of traffic, even in an overcrowded city like this.

The Old City? Possibly, and he could start there to eliminate it, but there was too much old magic there, and too many explorers looking for treasure amidst the junk. No, the Old City was far from overlooked.

There were a few places in the slums he could try, but... if he had to guess, he'd hazard that the curse was located somewhere easily overlooked but accessible to the caster. Somewhere they could go without anyone taking note, where they wouldn't be out of place. Not in a private residence, or even a public building, though, since those generally had either too much magic already that might affect the curse or had magic users living in or nearby who would notice the cantrip.

Trickier and trickier, but it also whittled down the options.

Unfortunately, it meant he'd have to cross the bridges to Westbridge, Rotter slang for the western half of the city where, aside for some slums right up on the river, only the well-heeled and wealthy lived. The biggest danger there was that if something went awry, he stood a good chance of being recognized. He'd just have to keep his mask firmly in place, avoid people as much as possible, and pray to the Eternal that nothing went too wrong.

Ha.

First thing was first, then. He needed clothes suitable to running around Westbridge. There was no way he'd go unremarked dressed as he was.

That meant paying a visit to Dawa.

After he was well clear of the Midden, Tashi looped back down the Sun, keeping close to the walls, well away from the open street where he was far more likely to be picked out of a crowd. Not that anyone was easily identified while wearing a mask, but the royal guards had plenty of magical tricks.

Close to the river, he turned down a narrow alleyway and banged on a creaky door just this side of falling apart. "Now, Dawa."

He heard scrambling, the rattle and clink as useless locks were undone, and finally the door swung open. "What?" Dawa asked, half-naked and flushed.

"Oh, sorry, did I interrupt something? Pay'em and toss'em."

Dawa sighed but didn't argue, merely vanished into the bedroom. A few minutes later a woman Tashi vaguely recognized as one of the regular hookers in the area came out, gave him a mocking salute, and departed.

"Now that you've ruined my afternoon plans," Dawa said as he came out of the bedroom, pulling on clothes and his hair still a mess, "what do you want?"

Tashi flipped a coin that Dawa deftly caught. "I need clothes suitable for blending into Westbridge."

"I think I've got some stuff. Come on." He picked up a ring of keys from a table by the bedroom door and crossed to the only door in the place that would take genuine effort to get into. Unlocking it, he retrieved a lantern from the floor, lit it, and vanished into the gloom beyond.

Being a healer, and other more sordid things, for the Rotter meant that Dawa was most often paid in goods rather than coin. When death was involved, payment was nearly always whatever the victim was wearing and had on them when they died, though Dawa was kinder than most in his profession in that he never took sentimental items; he always let the families keep those where desired.

Tashi followed him into the basement, down steps that creaked alarmingly. "You need to fix these steps."

"I don't need you telling me the obvious," Dawa said with a laugh. "I've been trying. It's always one problem after another." He lit some lamps around the room, revealing a veritable junkshop of belongings, tenuously organized into heaps by type.

Tashi went to the various piles of clothes and started sorting through them for an outfit suitable enough to let him wander through Westbridge unremarked. Eventually, he put together something that would make him look like a merchant who'd seen better days, definitely the sort to be unremarked and even ignored to a degree, as though the wealthy were afraid the loss of fortune was contagious.

When he was dressed in the new clothes, including a pair of shoes he managed to scrounge up, he turned to Dawa. "Can I leave my other things here and retrieve them later?"

"Sure, just put them in my room, otherwise some visitor or another will get sticky fingers."

Tashi obeyed, thanked Dawa again, and headed out.

On the street, he spied the prostitute he'd run out earlier, and flipped her a coin. "You can go back and finish the job if you want, sweetheart."

"Beats standing around here," she said, like Dawa wasn't one of the preferred clients, since he never asked for more than the services they provided and wasn't the type to beat or hurt them. An actual decent person, rare in the Rotter.

Tashi headed off toward Westbridge, fussing with his new, borrowed mask until it settled in place as well as it could without being tailored specifically to him. He missed his own, but if he was remarked on for anything at all, he didn't want the mask to be tied back to him.

Reaching Sunrise Boulevard again, he headed west across the bridge of the same name. There were three bridges in Ossiri: Sunrise and Moonrise, the largest and most frequently used, and then the Old Bridge, it's proper name long forgotten. It was the only one original to the Old City, smaller and weaker than its newer siblings, mostly used by work crews and the like. Traipsing across Old Bridge was a good way to get robbed at best and wind up another body in Oss at worst.

He stopped briefly along the way for food and ate hanging over the bridge so nothing would spill on his clothes. His stomach growled for more, but he'd already spent enough money that day, especially considering he couldn't get to his flat, which meant he couldn't reach his carefully hidden stash or see what new jobs waited for him. No income until this stupid problem was resolved.

Leave it to his family to be the reason he'd be flat broke and homeless not once, but twice.

On the other hand, he could charge an incredibly hefty fee for saving the life of the queen, and there was fuck all they'd be able to do about it, short of killing him outright, and both his mother and his sister preferred to just pay for problems to go away.

He really should have considered that sooner. What a cheering thought. The money he could demand, he wouldn't have to worry about anything for a long time.

As he reached the first major intersection on Westbridge, he lingered to decide where to start his search. Straight ahead would lead him to City Hall and the park right next to it, both viable places for hiding a powerful cantrip amidst so much other noise, though it would have to be heavily guarded to prevent interference from all the magic laid on City Hall. If he continued on west, he'd eventually pass through Swan Lake and onward to the royal palace. No, thank you.

Otherwise, he could head south to the business distract, where there was plenty of nooks and crannies where a cantrip might be tucked away, and certainly someone visiting that area at any given hour, even the dead of night, would not draw attention.

Of the two, the business distract was going to be the larger project, if not the most difficult, so Tashi went with that. If he didn't have any luck, he'd find somewhere to rest this side of the bridge tonight, and tomorrow tackle City Hall.

Far more likely, he'd spend two days coming up with a whole lot of nothing, and in the meantime, he wasn't getting actual work done, and ignoring the missives was going to tank his reputation, so that was lovely.

Nothing for it, though. He'd said he'd find the curse afflicting his damned mother and so he'd do it. They weren't going to like the bill he sent them, but that was too damned bad.

This would be so much easier with his rings, but Night forbid anybody make his job easier.

Chapter Seven

Turning down Harkit, he walked briskly toward the business distract, just one more busy person on the street. Paperboys shouted grossly exaggerated headlines, vendors called out the foods they were selling, and the people behind street stalls kept a sharp eye out for quick, sticky fingers,

All the food made his stomach growl, but Tashi pushed on. With all the jobs he was losing, he needed to save every coin he possibly could, or he was going to starve before he was able to take work again.

He stopped as he came to an alleyway that was particularly dark and narrow, and smelled like it had hosted more than a couple of corpses in its life. If only he could afford that bottle of mint oil. Maybe he'd just add it to his bill.

Thankfully, the only bodies he encountered as he prowled down the alley were those of rats and something so torn up he couldn't identify it. Hmm. Probably nothing, but he noted it anyway.

Halfway down the alleyway, he gently tested the metal ladder that had seen better days. It held, more or less, so he hefted himself up, going slowly, flinching at every creak and rattle. Just what he'd always wanted: to fall to his death from a rusty ladder, lying in pools of piss and shit and Night alone knew what else until someone bothered to have his corpse moved.

Why did anyone ever go up high on purpose? What was so wrong with staying on the damned ground?

Reaching the roof, he rested on his knees for a moment, drawing several breaths and carefully not looking anywhere that might reveal just how high up he was. And fine, it was 'only' two stories, but that was well over his limit of zero.

As long as he didn't look down, he'd be fine. Standing, Tashi moved to the center of the roof. He hadn't looked closely at the buildings on either side of the alley, but to judge by the smells and the sounds, he was standing on a perfume shop and next to a milliner.

Scrying for hidden magic would be a great

deal easier with the proper tools, but he wasn't bitter, not in the slightest. Rumér could have given him one ring, at the very least, but had he? No. Whatever. It was fine.

Extending his right hand, shoulders back, feet together, Tashi closed his eyes and concentrated. With his rings and a scrying crystal, he could have searched much farther and in greater detail, but he'd been trained by the best to someday *be* the best.

It was the only thing he really and truly missed about his old life. Even if it had been the duty assigned to him since birth, he loved magic with his whole heart.

He whispered the cantrip for finding, modified to look specifically for magic. The cantrip radiated out, coming back with various little charms to make life easier for the shopkeeps, the cantrips in the bowels of the city that kept everything running smoothly, or at least running.

There. Something that didn't belong. Oh, ho ho. Someone was using a love cantrip. Well, that was going to have to go. Tashi made note of where it was and finished out his cantrip. Nothing of curses. Not really surprising. He would have to do this five hundred times at least before he came across what he was looking for—assuming he found it all, given how well it had been hidden.

One problem at a time. Sweep the area first, then try another method.

First, of course, he had to get down.

Heights were great for widening the reach of things like finding a hidden curse, but that was about the only thing they were good for.

Gritting his teeth, and not looking down below, he swung out onto the ladder. His stomach churned, and his hands shook, but he could do this. He'd done it before, and it hadn't killed him. But the ladder was so rickety what if…

Nope. No. One step at a time. Rung, whatever.

He was about a third of the way down when a rung gave out beneath his boot, and he barely caught himself in time, heart pounding in his ears, a laugh-sob stuck in his throat. *Fuck* heights. *Fuck* this ladder. *Fuck* stupid Rumér for forcing him into this.

Still trembling, he finally resumed his climb down, fumbling briefly as he had to awkwardly move down to the next available rung, over the gap that had almost killed him.

Eventually, *finally*, he was back on solid ground. One ladder down, five million to go. Wonderful.

Tashi trudged out of the alley and continued on his way down the street. He whispered the finding cantrip again as he neared a candy shop, and sure enough, there was the love cantrip. Normally he'd let stray illegal spells be someone else's problem, but there were a handful he absolutely would not tolerate, and love cantrips were at the top of the list. They were ridiculously illegal, save for specific, tightly regulated uses—so illegal, they made body catching harmless by comparison.

The cantrip was inside the candy shop. Likely it was in a piece of merchandise. Strange they'd infect one item, or set of items, with an illegal cantrip but not others. Usually, these types were all in. Well, maybe they were testing the waters.

A bell over the door let out a silvery chime as he stepped inside, and he lifted a hand to the clerk behind the counter to signal he didn't require assistance just yet. The shop smelled of sugar and fruit, a faint hint of the lemon polish they used to keep the wood gleaming.

So much candy. Princess lollies. Caramels. Dragon drops. Gremlin bites. Tongue twisters. Cremes. Fizzies. Drop candies of every flavor; his favorite had always been lemon. Rainbow taffies, fairy clouds...

Tashi couldn't remember the last time he'd had a piece of candy. One of those things that you don't realize is a luxury until it's gone, until you realize that one bag or box of candy was a month's rent at least, or a month's worth of meals. Everything was counted in meals in the Rotter, meals and a place to sleep if you were lucky.

He browsed around the store, slowly working his way to the source of the magic, which proved to be the caramels, arranged in pretty gold trays behind glass. Calling up his magic, Tashi drew the cantrip in the air as he recited it, and with a soft purple glow, the love cantrip cast on the caramels broke and vanished.

"I beg your pardon, sir! What do you think you are doing?"

Tashi looked up, his smile all teeth as the clerk reached him. "Saving you from being shut down. If I find you breaking the law again, all they'll find of this place is ashes. Am I understood?"

The man, whose fine brown skin now looked more gray-yellow, gave a stiff not. "Yes, my lord."

"Have a nice day." Tashi departed, quietly mourning the loss of the bright, colorful shop and all its delightful treats, even though he had no interest in candy from a shop that would use love cantrips.

Sighing, he pressed on, heading to the next midpoint, climbing another terror-inducing ladder. Up and down he went, until he was sore and exhausted and so hungry his stomach would soon start eating itself.

So far, all he'd found was the candy shop love cantrip, two curses to cause irritating noise, and one alert cantrip that seemed meant to warn the woman of the house when her husband was approaching. He strengthened the alert cantrip, and left the noise-makers, mildly curious as to their purpose. Probably feuding neighbors. He'd once done something similar to annoy his eldest sister to death, and had been supremely put out when Rumér had made him take it down only a day later.

Tashi sat on a bench in a tiny scrap of park between a tailor and a shoe shop, yawning and rubbing his eyes. At least no one was chasing him today. For now, anyway.

Dusk had fallen, leaving the world washed in orange and purple, people rushing home to their suppers. Their families. Their cozy homes with warm fires and soft beds, blankets that weren't ridden with holes, where they didn't have to worry about fights or fires breaking out, or thieves trying to break into their room.

If he worked through the night, he could have the entire business distract searched before dawn. Then he could find somewhere to sleep and tackle City Hall when he woke, and then return to his room to properly rest and decide what to do next. Maybe contrive an actual plan.

His stomach rumbled, and he felt nauseous and headachey, visceral reminders that he hadn't had a real, full meal in a long time—but food cost money, and he didn't have much of that, and anyway, he couldn't afford anything on this side of the river. He could probably scrounge through the bins, but he hadn't been forced to do that for a long time, and he was going to start up again. Not yet, anyway.

Tashi pushed to his feet with a groan and continued on, slipping between the shoe shop and the leather goods store next to it that smelled nothing remotely like the tannery and workshop where all those costly leather goods were made by people who didn't make enough in a year to buy even one of the products they crafted nearly every single day.

He lived down the hall from a woman employed at the workshop. Every now and then he could hear her crying, trying to make her meager pay add up to money that was enough to take care of her and her daughter. Same story was scattered all over his building. Nothing he could do, though, except leave a coin or two in her mailbox when he could manage it.

Glaring at the ladder before him, daring the bastard to misbehave in even the slightest way, Tashi finally began his latest ascent. Unlike most of the buildings around here, this one was relatively new, and three stories high rather than two. The previous building had burned down when he was a child, a fire set by magic that had countered or blocked all the cantrips used to try to put the fire out. By the time they broke the magic, it was too late to save the building.

If only they'd been less ambitious in the rebuilding.

A rung creaked a little more than halfway up, and Tashi clung to the bars, accidentally saw how high up he was, and pinched his eyes shut with a whimper. Why couldn't everything just be on the fucking ground? There was plenty of land,

and no logical reason at all for building things so high.

He was going to throw up, and it was going to be awful because his stomach wasn't filled with anything except terror and hunger.

By the time he reached the top and crawled onto the roof, he was trembling so badly all he could do was sit huddled against the high ledge that surrounded the roof, arms across his spread knees, head on his arms, gulping in air and willing himself to calm down. Night, he fucking *hated* this.

Why couldn't someone else do this? Why did he always have to do it alone?

Whatever. That was stupid thinking. He'd been fine on his own, ever since he'd learned the hard way that he'd never really had anyone else. That he'd never truly *had* anyone else.

All right. Enough with behaving like a pathetic child. Time to get back to work. Tashi pushed slowly to his feet, keeping his eyes firmly down as he walked to the center of the roof. At least from this high up, the finding cantrip would ripple out even farther, cutting his work down significantly.

Taking a deep breath, Tashi drew himself up into position and cast the cantrip.

Nothing but more petty nonsense. Someone had set a mouse-attracting curse behind the leather shop. A curse for foul odors lingered outside the cologne shop a short ways down. More alert cantrips, some to warn people to toss their lovers, but others would have more practical use, like to assist the blind, deaf, and similar such.

Any ordinary day, he might mess with the petty ones just to see the resulting chaos, and if he had the strength left he'd bolster the actually useful, important ones like he had for that poor woman afraid of her husband.

Hmm… there was an interesting curse. Why would someone…

DONG!

Tashi jerked so hard he nearly toppled himself, the cantrip falling away as his concentration shattered. He stared in annoyance and confusion as the great bells of City Hall continued to toll. Not the emergency toll, but of importance all the same. Anyone who was able was to report to the plaza to hear an announcement, or receive special orders, or whatever Her Majesty decided was worth interrupting everyone's day.

Probably had nothing to do with the Rotter, and if his mother had died, they would be ringing the mourning bells. Not something he had to care about then, except for caring that it stopped so he could get back to work.

The bells didn't stop though, they tolled on and on, as if determined to make certain that every last person in the city was inconvenienced. Despite himself, Tashi grew curious—worried. With all the upheaval lately, it would be his luck if this was one more part of the problem.

Fine. Whatever. He'd go.

Ugh, first he had to deal with the ladder again. Muttering several choice blasphemies, he made his way to the ladder and slowly down it, trembling every step of the way, breathing haggard, eyes pinched shut. Getting back on solid ground took entirely too long.

And still the bells tolled.

Mouth tight with growing trepidation, Tashi headed off, moving his way quickly west and then north until he came to the already-crowded plaza in front of City Hall. He pushed and shoved and occasionally outright cheated with whispered cantrips to make his way to the front.

When he finally broke through the crowd, he nearly *did* throw up the non-existent contents of his stomach.

Ezhil and Vyra, manacled and on their knees on a dais, muting collars locked around their throats. Like they were fucking animals. Because that was all Westbridge saw when they looked at the Rotter. Animals.

Standing in front of them, clearly waiting for the crowd to reach a level she found acceptable, was his sister. Crown Princess Janashta Hashar herself, dark skin gleaming with a delicate touch of moondust, precious jewels in her long, braided hair, her stupid tiara firmly in place, in her full military-style regalia so she'd look that much more intimidating, complete with that stupid half-cloak she loved so much, trimmed in yeti fur, so rare and precious that one length of it could feed his entire building for a year.

He'd once had a cowl made of the same, dyed dark blue and set with pearls. It had been his favorite thing to wear in the winter months. Now the idea of such wasteful clothing made him nauseous. It was so fucking *stupid.*

She wasn't wearing a mask, but he could see it strapped to her belt, silk and velvet and glittering jewels, so she must have been wearing it until recently.

As the crowd finally reached a crescendo, she signaled the men stationed at one corner of the dais, who banged on enormous drums until silence fell.

"Good people of Ossiri, I require your assistance on a matter most grave. We are seeking a man who attempted to murder a member of my family. He hides in this city, likely desperate to escape. Two of his conspirators are here. It's believed he works as a wretched, so-called body catcher. He uses magic illegally. Be careful and keep your eyes sharp for anyone who looks out of place. My good soldiers will be handing out descriptions as you depart."

She continued speaking, but Tashi had lost all interest. They were accusing *him* of murder? Like, yes, he'd killed one person and that bastard had deserved it, but they really thought after all this time he'd waste his time and effort trying to kill the family that had tossed him out? He had better things to do, and what would killing them accomplish? He wasn't a woman; it was highly unlikely he'd ever be granted the throne, even if he wanted it. He'd been disowned and thrown out.

Whatever. That didn't matter. He could handle his fucking sister. His only real worry was for Ezhil and Vyra, who shouldn't be mixed up in this at all. Ezhil was a shithead, but he didn't deserve this, and Vyra was far too kind to be anywhere near the Rotter. He'd thought running off would keep them safe, but he had grossly miscalculated.

Tashi would be damned if they were made casualties of his family's drama. The only question, then, was the best way to get them free. Turn himself in, see what his sister was really up to? Or wait until later that night and try to break them free?

Damn it, why wasn't Rumér doing something about her? Surely he'd told her he had the matter well in hand. Did his sister really think he was responsible for the stupid curse? Not really his style, and she of all people should know that.

Turning himself in might give him a chance at the resources he badly needed to find the curse. It could also get him dead once and for all, or worse locked up indefinitely, left to rot, what little life he'd managed to scrape out gone forever.

If he waited, though, it was possible an opportunity would never present itself, and his friends would be dragged away, sentenced, and left to languish or die in whatever miserable sentence they were handed.

Ugh, he'd just called Ezhil his friend. Fuck everything.

Night, what in the world was he supposed to do? He had no good options here.

Focus, he needed to focus.

Right. If he turned himself in, he'd probably be killed, and they'd probably kill Ezhil and Vyra for the sake of thoroughness. So turning himself in just wasn't an option. He'd have to figure out how to get them free.

With no help. No supplements to his magic. Against the royal guard.

Should be a fucking lark.

Chapter Eight

Tashi turned away, weaving and shoving back through the crowd, until he finally had some space to breathe and think.

All right, his worthless sister was using Ezhil and Vyra to bait him, which meant she'd want them under her thumb the whole time. So she was more than likely going to keep them imprisoned at the palace.

So he would need to get into the palace or intercept them before that point. Intercepting them would provide a far better chance of success, but there were any number of routes they could take back to the palace, or any combination of them precisely to circumvent such shenanigans. He also doubted he could take on the entire escort by himself, even with his magic. Their mages wouldn't be better, but they would be better equipped and stronger.

Tashi walked until he came to a quiet street, then slipped down an alleyway and picked the lock on the door of a business that was closed for the day. Inside, he found more than he could have hoped for: an empty office, with all the writing supplies he could ever need; a basket of food either forgotten or meant to be eaten the next day; and peace and quiet.

Sitting down with the food, Tashi lit a couple of lamps, pulled out paper and pen, and set to work. He first roughed out a map of the city, followed by marking out all the viable routes, which as he'd already known, was overwhelming. There was no way to safely guess which streets they'd take, if they'd double back, make needless turns and loops…

His only chance would be the sole chokepoint in the mess: the Boulevard of Fallen Stars that led directly to the palace. Initially built and used for troop movement, these days it was just the showy runner leading to the palace, as gilded and overdramatic as everything else on that end of the city.

Unfortunately, proximity to the royal palace meant it was heavily fortified, with magic and troop presence. Hmm…

Tashi considered and discarded one idea after another, until he was left with only one:

chaos. His best chance of getting to them, and getting them out again, was unmitigated chaos.

He nibbled on bread with butter and sourberry jam, interspersed with bites of sharp cheese and salty olives, while he pondered his options. Fire was too dangerous and uncontrollable. He wanted chaos, not destruction.

Hmm…

Pulling out the small bottle of wine in the basket, Tashi opened it and took a deep pull. Sweet wine, good contrast to the savory and salty that made up most of the basket.

Sadly, all the best distractions required things he didn't have: time and money. Well, sometimes the oldest methods worked the best: when it doubt, start a fight. Pissing people off was reliable, cheap and easy, and after they got going, good luck stopping them.

He poked around his borrowed office, which seemed to belong to an herbalist, for some useful odds and ends that included mint oil, which improved his mood significantly. He tucked his prizes away in his pockets and pouches as he finished the wine. He ran through a mental list of the best shops and cafés to hit, mapping out the order and what exactly he would do. There'd be significant property damage, but well, they shouldn't have kidnapped his friends over something that wasn't even his fault.

This was what he got for agreeing to help at all.

As ready as he would ever be, Tashi tidied the office up, put the empty basket back where he'd found it, helped himself to the small bag of coins stashed in the hidden drawer of the desk, and headed out.

He took side streets and alleyways, a meandering path to the Boulevard that would make it difficult for any sharp eyes to pinpoint for the guards where he'd been going or to what purpose. He could have been anyone doing anything, the kind of person that eyes slid over a hundred times a day.

Once upon a time, all eyes had been on him when he entered a room and he'd known it. Nowadays, he hated to be anything but invisible. No thanks to his sister, soon everyone in the Rotter would hear the description of the person she was seeking, and more than a few of them would be happy to turn him in at a chance for good coin. So now he'd lost his safety and his income. He'd lost *everything*.

His stupid sister was definitely going to pay for that.

One thing at a time. Right now, his only priority was saving Ezhil and Vyra, who never should have been caught up in this mess. Not even Ezhil, who generally deserved every wrong dropped on his head, the infuriating, know-it-all bastard.

Who by now knew with absolutely no shadow of a doubt that Tashi was indeed the long-missing Prince Tenzin. So probably Vyra knew it too. Marvelous. Clearly his only choice when this current mess was sorted was to leave the city. Rumér would just have to find the curse on his own, and damn Tashi for agreeing to help.

Once he reached the Boulevard, the first thing Tashi did was go in search of sewer entrances. Here they were all accessed by way of circular holes cut into the street and covered with heavy metal lids. Normally a special hook was required to lift them, but he'd be coming up from beneath, so that was a moot point. At worst, he could use a cantrip for lightness. This wasn't quite dead center of the street, and it was right in the midst of the chaos he planned to cause, so perfect.

From there, he retraced his steps until he came to one of the sewer entrances on a smelly off street, behind a restaurant that boasted fresh fish but smelled like the refuse from the canning factory.

Here, the entrance was a steep set of stairs that led down to a creaky metal door that no one had even bothered to lock. From there… well, it was hardly the first time Tashi had traipsed about the sewers, and it wouldn't be the last.

A soft cantrip brought up a couple of mage lights, and every few steps he created a new, small one to guide his path to and from the sewer entrance beneath the Boulevard. Once that was done, he returned to the surface and made his way back to the Boulevard, stopping only to cast a quick cantrip to banish any suspicious, attention-catching smells.

Back on the Boulevard, he took a leisurely stroll down one end and up the other, marking the buildings that would be most ideal for causing chaos. Once his initial sweep was done, he made a second loop, this time to put his cantrips in place—for noise, for flashes of light, for illusions of breaking and spilling, voices calling insults and epithets.

The entire debacle would be crude but effective. He placed twice what he needed, on the chance some of them failed or were discovered before they could be activated, then bought some more food with his stolen coin and sat on a bench to enjoy it while he waited.

He could not remember the last time he'd had such decadent food, from the basket of goodies stolen earlier to the flaky, buttery pastries he was eating now, two with savory fillings of minced lamb, potatoes and carrots and fragrant spices, and one sweet filled with lemon cream. He topped it all with coffee, hot and fresh with just a touch of cream.

Food was about the only thing he missed from his old life, other than all the supplements for his magic that he could sorely use right now. Well, and a comfortable bed, but honestly, none of that was worth going back for. Especially not for his shithead sister accusing him of attempted murder. She kept it up, she was gonna see completed murder.

He'd just finished his coffee, and was pondering a second cup, when guards came into view and started quietly ushering people off the streets. Tashi didn't wait for them to speak to him directly, simply slipped away to the sewer entrance by the restaurant. Climbing down into the stinking dark, he followed his mage lights back to the Boulevard and climbed the ladder up to the street.

A quick cantrip lifted one edge of the sewer cover just enough for him to see the street, right as the expected escort appeared. What he *hadn't* expected was that they'd put his friends in a fucking cage—a glorified cart with iron bars all around it, like they were dangerous criminals who needed constant supervision.

Rage boiled through Tashi, but he tamped it down. If his sister wanted a reckoning, she was going to fucking get it—but not right now. His only goal right now was to get his friends to safety, to ensure they wouldn't be troubled by him and his family drama ever again. Which meant never seeing them again, a thought which shouldn't hurt as much as it did. He didn't even like Ezhil, and he barely knew Vyra.

Whatever. He needed to focus. The cage was an added challenge, but not insurmountable. He saw no sign of his sister, but that wasn't really surprising; she'd probably taken a different route, so royalty and prisoners were not in the same high-risk place. She hadn't come this way already, so either she was coming this way after the prisoners were safely within the palace walls, or she was taking a completely different route that avoided the Boulevard, which was annoying and difficult and not really like her.

Well, didn't matter, not right now.

Tashi took a deep breath, then whispered the activations for his cantrips.

Everything was quiet at first, and then noisy—and then it was like a bursting dam, with shouts and screaming, running and fighting, horses and soldiers panicking as everyone tried to figure out what was going on and how it had all gone wrong.

Tashi shoved the sewer cover aside and hefted himself up, keeping low as he threaded through the chaos, tossing out cantrips to drop guards as he was able, because even one less guard to deal with would make all the difference in the world.

Reaching the cage, he set to work on the various levels of protection.

"Took you long enough, Your Highness," Ezhil said.

"Not now," Tashi hissed.

"Behind!" Vyra said.

Tashi whipped around just in time to avoid taking a brutal blow to the head, ducking and sinking a fist into the stupid guard's gut. Not that it had much impact with the leather armor he wore, but it was enough to throw the bastard off balance, which was all Tashi needed for a quick cantrip.

He returned to work on the locks, which had an unnecessary numbers of layers of magic on them—but nothing he couldn't handle in the end, though there were a few more interruptions before he was done.

Thankfully, his chaos plan had worked well, even with the guards clearing streets beforehand. There were always gawkers, after all, subtle and not, and it only took two to start a fight.

"Come on," he hissed as he finally got the door open. "The sewers. Dead ahead."

"Ugh," Ezhil said, but bolted obediently in the direction he'd indicated.

"Down!" Vyra snarled, and swung a fist as Tashi obediently ducked, sending a guard flying from the force of his blow.

Tashi whistled in appreciation, but before he could comment, they were running again, all but diving into the sewer entrance. He clung to the ladder and cast the cantrip that slid the lid back in place, then used another one to ensure the lid was too heavy for anyone to be lifting anytime soon.

"Follow the lights!" he called out, then hastened down the ladder to catch up to the other two, chest heaving, breaths coming in hot, lung-burning gulps.

He bent, hands on his knees, as they finally reached the stairs up to the door by the restaurant, gulping desperately for more air, no matter how foul it was. So long as he didn't think too hard about what he was inhaling, it was fine.

"We should stay down here," Vyra said. "We go up, they'll find us for sure, but hopefully nobody really noticed us going down here, which gives us an edge."

"Agreed," Ezhil said. "Come on, I know my way around this place more than I like. You'd be surprised how often people just throw bodies down here thinking they'll never be found, like every other joe and jenny in the city hasn't had the exact same thought."

"I'm too tired right now, but remind me to mock you mercilessly later for that," Tashi said. "Lead the way, by all means. I certainly wasn't able to plan further than breaking you free, which worked better than I expected, to be perfectly honest. I thought my—the guards would be better prepared than that. Whatever, though. Worked out for us."

Vyra gave him a curious look, brow furrowing, and Tashi turned away, cringing inwardly. Of course, all that did was put him in direct sight of Ezhil's knowing smirk. "Shut up. I'm serious. One word and I will knock you right into that ominous brown sludge trudging by us."

"Yes, Your Highness."

"Can we get moving please?"

Ezhil rolled his eyes. "Jump over the brown sludge and follow that white line on the wall until

I tell you to stop. Can you bring up more of your lights?"

"Of course I can. Mage lights are children's work." He created a glowing orb for each of them, casting them out to rest at about shoulder height, lending plenty of guidance as they trudged their way through the dark, damp, putrid sewers.

They walked in silence for several minutes, sharing the occasional grimace over a particularly awful stench or the occasional remains, human and other. Sometimes, there was no discerning what in the Night they were looking at, and Tashi fervently hoped he never found out.

"I'm sorry for all this," he said eventually. "You two never should have been caught up in my drama. I thought if I left, you'd be safe. I hope they didn't hurt you too much."

"We're fine," Vyra said. "Little roughed up, but that happens on the daily in the Midden. Street thugs hit way harder than any soft guard."

Ezhil snorted. "What *is* your drama, Your Highness? Did you really kill someone? Not judging mind, a few of the bodies I've buried were my own handiwork, but sounds like you killed the Queen herself." He laughed—and faltered at whatever he saw on Tashi's face. "Holy Night, did you really?"

"No," Tashi hissed. "It's a long story, but if you really want to hear it, I'll tell it. Not here, though, please."

"Don't worry, we're almost to our

destination."

"My sister, will she be all right?" Vyra asked.

"Yes, she will be," Tashi said. "If my—Her Highness had any interest in taking your sister as well, she would have already. She probably realizes it wouldn't be a good look to harm a woman who once spent time in an asylum, given all the drama going on amongst the Uppers about it ever since they found the body dump in Swallowtail."

"Your what?" Vyra asked. "You've done that twice."

"Nothing," Tashi relied.

"His sister," Ezhil said. "His fucking sister, isn't that right, *Your Highness*."

Vyra's eyes widened. *"What."*

Tashi glared murder. "You need to shut the fuck up, you shit-for-brains. Your mouth is exactly why you're always in trouble."

Ezhil smirked and looked over his shoulder to bat his eyes ridiculously. "My mouth also gets me out of trouble."

"I sincerely doubt it."

Vyra laughed. "Things can't be too awful if the pair of you are right back to your antics."

Ezhil made a face and turned back around. "Here we go. This way." He veered off down a narrow tunnel, then led them up a rickety ladder covered in things Tashi carefully avoided thinking about or looking at too closely.

After they reached the top, and once he'd slid the cover back into place, Tashi gulped in fresh air until he was practically dizzy with it. "Please tell me there's a way to get clean in our near future."

"Oh, definitely, though you're not going to like the first round."

"I really don't care, as long as I stop *smelling*. Even the Rotter has some standards."

Ezhil laughed and led them down what proved to be the wide alleyway between two rows of houses where delivery carts and the like would come to drop things at the back gates, so as not to muss the front entrance with their grimy presence.

About two-thirds of the way down, he stopped at a gate and made swift work of the lock, ushering them through before closing and locking it again behind them. "This way." When they'd reached the yard proper, grass turning to smooth stone where laundry and other chores that made a mess would be done, he added, "Wait here, I'll be back in a few."

Tashi immediately sat down, more than happy to hold still for a bit after a long day of moving, moving, and more moving.

"Is it true, what he said?" Vyra asked softly. "Are you really that prince that went missing forever ago?"

"I was that prince, yes," Tashi said, unable to keep all the bitterness from his voice. "That was a long fucking time ago, and I'm not that person anymore. If I'm lucky, I never will be again. The more time passes, the less I like him." He glared at where Ezhil had vanished. "I don't know how the fuck he figured it out."

Vyra chuckled. "I get the impression that being too smart for his own good is a big source of Ezhil's problems."

"I'm pretty sure the main source is his mouth."

Vyra laughed more loudly at that, but before he could reply, Ezhil returned. "All clear. Come on." He led the over to a water pump and started to strip. "Rinse off out here, then we'll get proper baths in the kitchen. Leave the clothes; I'll burn them in the morning."

Tashi groaned, but otherwise obeyed without complaint, putting his belongings in a small pile before stripping off his filthy, sodden clothes and tossing them in a different pile. Once they were clean, and Tashi's balls had tried to climb back up into his body from the sheer iciness of the pump water, they hastened into the house. Next to the enormous fireplace, big enough to spit roast several full-sized geese at once, was a couple of large wash basins. Taking them down, they worked to fill them as quickly as they could, and a quick cantrip was all it took to get the water nice and hot.

They took it in turns to scrub in the first bin and rinse off in the second. Wrapped in drying sheets that Ezhil had gotten from who knew where, Tashi and Vyra followed him down a couple of hallways, threading through the servant quarters of a clearly impressive city manor, to a small room filled with junk—including trunks that would likely contain old clothes. "Get dressed, then we'll get food and start talking."

Chapter Nine

Tashi regarded the three trunks in front of him: a blue one, a green one, and a black one. Yawning, he went to the blue trunk first, picking the half-hearted lock easily before throwing open the top. Instead of clothes, he was greeted with a pile of junk.

"This one is all gowns; not terribly practical right now," Ezhil said, and slammed the red trunk closed again.

Tashi cast him a look. "That makes it sound like you wear a gown from time to time."

"Maybe," Ezhil muttered, and if Tashi didn't know better, he'd swear Ezhil's cheeks were flushed. "What's it to you?"

"Nothing at all," Tashi said, because it was

true. He had no interest whatsoever in seeing Ezhil dolled up in a gown.

He put his mind back on the blue trunk before it betrayed him. "This one is all junk." He crouched in front of it anyway, poking through the odds and ends: old linens; cheap candlesticks that had seen better days; some broken glass that made the whole trunk smell of old, cheap perfume… and a small leather purse at the very bottom, shoved into a corner. It was grimy, covered in dust and who knew what else, reeking of the bad perfume… but it jingled promisingly as he picked it up.

Pulling it open, he tipped several coins onto the floor. Silver, every last one of them. More money than he'd seen since he'd been thrown out. "Well, looks like we won't need to worry about funds for a while." Between this and the coins he'd stolen from the office, money, for once, wasn't something he needed to worry about. He divided the coins into three piles, giving the single extra coin to Vyra. Scooping them up, he dispersed the piles and joined Vyra at the only trunk that seemed to hold clothes that would be of any use to them.

Thankfully, the trunk was large and held a vast store of discarded clothes in various sizes, all of them a season or three out of fashion, but it wasn't like he was about to show up to tea with his mother, was it?

Once he was finally dressed, in dark gray

breeches just a smidge too tight and a white shirt just slightly too big, with a blue and silver waistcoat that actually fit perfectly somehow, he turned to the far more difficult task of shoes. Ezhil managed to find a good pair of boots, the lucky bastard, leaving Vyra with some old working boots that had clearly been tossed for a reason, and Tashi with fancy buckled shoes better suited to a ballroom. Overall, he looked like he'd gotten dressed in the dark. Oh, well, running for his life hardly required looking smart.

"Can we have food now?" Vyra asked. "I'll leave all my shiny new coins for it if I have to."

Ezhil snorted. "Keep the coins, you silly Midden. The people who live here won't even notice it's gone. Their staff might, and you can bet they'll replace it without saying a single damn word."

"How do you know this place so well?" Tashi asked as they headed back the way they'd come to return to the kitchen. "I'll make tea."

Ezhil didn't reply, simply vanished into the larder, making several trips as he brought out food enough to feed twenty. When the food was arranged and the tea made, they sat down and dug in. "All right, Your Highness. Let's have it. Why is such a fuss being made of you suddenly?"

"Why do I have to do story time first?" Tashi muttered.

"You're the reason we need to have a story time at all," Ezhil retorted.

Tashi grimaced, conceding the point. "Fine. Yes, I was once Prince Tenzin, meant to someday serve as Warlock Prime to my sister, Crown Princess Janashta. Then I killed a powerful visiting dignitary, a man powerful enough that my murdering him could have very likely started a war. He and I had been bickering and fighting all that past week, ever since he showed up thinking he was the greatest thing to ever be born, when thank you, that title *clearly* belonged to me."

"I cannot picture you as a peacocking palace swain," Vyra said.

Ezhil rolled his eyes and said, "I can," before biting into a sausage.

"Oh, shut up," Tashi muttered. "Anyway, one night I caught him harassing a young woman, and by harassing, I mean attempting to rape. She was the youngest daughter of yet another visiting dignitary. I was drunk, angry, and hoping to impress her because what peacock isn't always looking to impress? Mostly I was angry, because even an atrociously spoiled brat like me could see that some actions, some crimes, are unforgivable." He glared at the table as memories he'd buried years came surging back to the fore of his mind. "The fight was ugly, because peacocks we might have been, we both knew how to fight. The girl was able to flee, which was all that mattered to me, but he wouldn't let the matter drop. We completely destroyed the room where it all happened. Then... to this day I don't know what exactly happened. He had me pinned, left bruises on my throat he was choking me so tightly. I wrested him off, punched him, then shoved him again. He stumbled, or tripped, and his head cracked right into the corner of the fireplace mantel. He didn't get back up."

There'd been blood and more on the mantel. Tashi had managed to hold himself together then, but later in his room he'd thrown up until there was nothing in his stomach and his throat burned.

"A guard found us first. He sent immediately for my mother, who had me locked in my room until the mess was cleaned up. After everything was over, and most of the palace was asleep, she had the guards escort me from the palace and told me on no uncertain terms that I was no longer her son, and if I tried to do anything other than walk away, I'd be killed on the spot. Here I am."

"Mother of All," Vyra said. "What happened with the dead dignitary, the girl you saved?"

"I have no idea. My mother told me it was no longer my concern. She let me keep the clothes I was wearing, which weren't terribly useful for surviving on the street. That's how I met Dawa, actually. He saw my clothes and offered to trade me them for something more practical. Never asked any questions."

Vyra shook his head. "How did you

survive?"

"By whoring—how else?" Tashi replied bitterly. "One night, after about eight months on the street, I came across a couple of young girls who'd accidentally killed their abusive mother trying to fight her off. It resonated, obviously, so I helped them get rid of the body. I'd only sort of heard of body catchers until that night. When those girls had a friend who needed help, they contacted me again, and the rest is for the bards, as they say. I've been a body catcher ever since." He shrugged one shoulder and refilled his teacup. "Not really an interesting tale in the end."

"Says the disowned prince on the run from his sister, accused of yet another murder, hiding away with a feral and a body snatcher after rescuing them mere steps from the palace," Ezhil said with a snort. "You're something else, Your Highness."

"All right, it's your turn, you loud-mouthed ass end of a goat," Tashi snapped, setting his cup down sharply. "How in the Night did you figure it out? How do you know about this house, that it would have everything we need and be safe to lurk in tonight?"

Ezhil shrugged. "I'm a body snatcher. You know how many of these uppities need bodies for things I prefer not to ask about? Mostly for their fancy schooling, but also for things I'm careful to keep ignorant about. Pretty sure the man down the street in the red house just likes collecting them or something. Anyway, this is one of the medical clients. Always buying up bodies for 'research'. He's out of the country right now, and the family that stayed behind went to their country manor for the rest of the year." He shook his head. "I can't imagine what it would be like to own multiple houses. I can barely afford my little hole in the attic." That infuriating smirk appeared. "How many houses did you own?"

"None, they all belong to the ruling monarch. Last I knew, my mother had twenty-seven residences. I have no doubt the number's gone up by now. Seriously, tell me how the fuck you figured it out."

"It was something you said, way back when we first met. Well, that something you said brought a lot of little pieces together, I should say. The way you spoke, the way you moved, your accent when you really get riled up... do you remember when we met?"

Tashi gave a single, sharp laugh. "It would be hard to forget. I was showing up to retrieve a body, and you were delivering one. I still don't understand why that dumbass didn't have you do the delivery and the hauling."

"Because he's a stupid drivel-driven twat like you, with all that 'rest in peace' nonsense. I bring him bodies nobody claims, he does his creepy experiments, then you take them away for a proper burial. He's good money, though, so whatever."

Vyra looked between them, mouth curving into a slow grin. "Did you two get into a fight?"

"I don't know how you guessed," Tashi replied dryly. "He was a smarmy little jackass encroaching on my job."

"You were a snotty know-it-all encroaching on *my* job, is what you mean," Ezhil said, lips twitching.

Rolling his eyes, Vyra said, "I see you learned nothing about staying out of fights."

"Look, in my defense, spoiled brats take longer than twelve months to break the worst of their habits, and I'd only just stopped being a whore at that point." Tashi made a face. "I was… concerned… that this encroaching little fuckhead was going to steal what little money I was making. I didn't want to go back to the life I'd just escaped." To whoring for cretins who treated him like a thing. To being constantly hungry and thirsty. Sleeping wherever he best had a chance of not being woken by frogs or raped by a desperate bastard sensing easy prey.

About the only thing he hadn't been reduced to was selling himself to the workhouses or a ship, which would have guaranteed a swift and likely painful death. Sad day when whoring was a better and safer option than mind-numbing work.

Ezhil grimaced as he stole the last sausage. "Yeah, had the ol' turn whore or go to the workhouse stint myself, but it was nine months.

I'm not sure there's a soul in the Rotter who hasn't walked that road. It's almost a rite of passage."

"That's the depressing truth," Tashi said.

"All the same to you, I'll keep trying to avoid it," Vyra said. "Pretty as the pair of you are, I'm surprised you didn't just take over a brothel or something with your popularity."

Ezhil smirked. "I had offers from a few."

"We both have too many attitude problems for a lifelong career in pleasing people," Tashi retorted.

Ezhil and Vyra laughed. "Fine, fine, you might have a point, Your Highness."

"Stop calling me that, please," Tashi said. "I'm not a prince anymore, and it's clear I was never fit for the title anyway. I hate hearing it."

"Ugh, fine, but that just means I'm going to come up with something worse."

"Seriously, though, how did you figure it out?"

"That first time we met, you called me a knob-knocker, which wasn't an insult I'd ever heard in my life. I eventually figured out it was a term used by Westside uppities. Thought that was weird, but didn't think much of it. But you get *really* mad your poncy accent comes out, and one night when he was drunk Dawa showed me those fancy clothes you gave him in exchange for normal clothes. Wasn't hard to put it all together."

Tashi sighed. "I hate you. I hate you so fucking much. Why did I save your dumb ass from those frogs." He ate the last of his cheese and buttered a slice of bread. "How did you wind up a whore when your family owns one of the most popular restaurants in the Rotter?"

"My mother, who owned it previously, had a gambling problem. Same as a thousand other dumbasses in this city. Popular wasn't enough to fix the problems she left when she croaked. Our little friend here ain't the only one thinks I'm pretty, so whoring it was, until like you, I kind of stumbled into snatching. Whoring was easier, but strangely, carting around dead bodies is safer."

Vyra shook his head. "I'm starting to feel like the most boring man at the table. There's no story worth telling in my history. I worked doing grimy jobs back home; I do them here. Only difference is that here nobody thinks my sister needs to be beaten and locked away for daring to speak her mind."

"What?" Ezhil stared at him blankly. "What in the world are you talking about?"

"Ferals are a patriarchal culture," Tashi replied. "Women are expected to be quiet, obedient, and pleasant at all times. It's kind of an old joke, how badly they react when they visit Valithta, which is matriarchal."

"Stop using your fancy fucking words, ponce."

Tashi lobbed the end of the loaf of bread at him. "In feral society, the men are in charge. Valithta, the women are in charge." He was also certain Ezhil understood the word choices just fine—but less certain that Vyra did, which was probably why Ezhil had spoken up.

Night, he was tired. "Are we safe here for the night?"

"Probably shouldn't linger overlong, I'm sure your sister has all sorts of fancy mages looking for us, but a couple of hours of rest probably won't hurt. Though once we're out of town, I have no idea where to go. I've never left the city."

Vyra set his cup of tea down. "I might be able to help with that. At the very least I can give us a destination and a place to resupply before we have to move."

"Send word to me when you're safe," Tashi said.

They stared at him, then Ezhil scowled. "What do you mean? You're not coming with us?"

"I may not be the one trying to kill my mother, but someone is. She's been cursed, and it's somewhere in this city, and right now, I'm the only one who can find it, and I won't clear my name otherwise. I'd also like to know what Rumér learns about my poor little sister." At their baffled expressions, Tashi told that story too. By the time he was done, all he wanted was to crawl into the nearest bed and remain there indefinitely. "So as you can see, I can't just leave, and even if I could, my going with you will just get you captured again, or even killed."

"Fuck all that," Ezhil said. "You don't have to clear your name or anything else. Do you remember the part where you told us they disowned you? Threw you out on the street with nothing but the clothes you wore? You must not have been wearing even jewelry, because jewelry like you must have worn back then would have set you up nicely. Your putrid cunt of a sister just had us arrested over nothing, all to draw you out because she's accusing you of murder with no proof whatsoever. Fuck them. That's not how family acts, and if they're not going to act like family, they sure as fuck don't deserve to be treated like family. Who gives a fuck if your name is cleared? If you leave, it won't ever matter."

"Agreed." Vyra sat back in his seat and folded his arms across his chest, regarding Tashi pensively. "You don't owe them a damn thing. While I can understand why you'd want to at least hear what happened to your little sister... you probably can't, simple as that. Unless you want to go back to that world, which it sounds like you don't. I know you don't like it when I agree with the snatcher," he added with a faint smile, "but you don't owe anything to people who left you to die on the streets. Come with us, and if you really want to get involved in this stupid mess... well, come back. After proper rest and shit, where you were able to think and plan in safety." He lifted a hand when Tashi started to protest. "As to doing it to protect us, we're adults. We can make our own decisions and look after ourselves—well, mostly. I admit I wasn't prepared for getting arrested by the royal guard and dragged off to be made a spectacle of. But I don't see that happening twice. It's not your place to decide what risk we take. Come with us, that's what we both want."

Tashi hated to admit they were right, mostly because he hated to admit Ezhil could ever be right about anything. On the other hand, he couldn't just ignore someone was trying to murder the queen, and his sister thought that someone was him. If he left now, he could just be making everything worse.

Why did his choices always seem to come down to either fight a losing battle or run away? He was so tired of those being the only options in his life. He'd managed to carve out a relatively stable life for himself. He'd been bothering no one, had wanted nothing except to be left in peace. Yet here he was again, completely fucked because of other people, and once more forced to decide if he was going to stay or if he was going to go.

Chapter Ten

"All right," he finally said.

"All right?" Ezhil echoed.

"I'll go. You're right, as much as I'd rather die than admit that, you toad-licker. Let's get out of this fucking city before they find us again."

To his complete astonishment, Ezhil and Vyra broke into matching smiles, and damned if he didn't like knowing he'd pleased them. Made them happy. Ugh, had he really sunk so low he was looking to Ezhil for a good opinion now? Maybe he should have let his sister have him.

Standing, he gathered up the dirty dishes and carried them over to the wash tub, which thankfully was connected to plumbing, sparing him having to go out into the yard to pump water.

"Never thought I'd see a prince washing dishes," Ezhil said, and laughed when Tashi cast him a nasty look over his shoulder. "Then again, never thought I'd have a prince regularly calling me..." He lifted one hand and started ticking epithets off as he listed them, "...goat fucker, toad licker, rancid ballsack, pus-riddled dick, bone-banger, sister-fucker... huh, you really do spend a lot of time thinking about me fucking things. I'm a bit concerned about your proclivities though, Your Highness."

"If you don't shut the fuck up, I'm going to dunk your head in this water and leave it there indefinitely." Tashi finished the washing and dried his hands on a cloth hanging on the wall behind the tub. "So where can we sleep for a couple of hours?" Doing magic all day had him wrung out, never mind everything else that had happened.

Ezhil rose to his feet with an easy elegance that didn't seem fair after the long day they'd had. "This way." He led them back down the hallways they'd used before, but turned opposite the direction of the room where the trunks had been, then up a short flight of stairs that turned sharply at the halfway point, and finally down another short hallway to the room at the end.

Inside were four beds, so small he'd fall off if he turned or shifted without thinking, but everything smelled of clean linens and a faint hint of lavender. At the end of the day, food in your belly and a clean, warm bed was all that really mattered.

Going to one of the beds nearest the door, so he'd be between it and the other two should anyone bother them, he sat on the edge and pulled off his socks and shoes, then stripped down to his breeches and hung the rest of his clothes on the hooks by the bed intended for that purpose.

Last of all, he drew a quick cantrip in the air, and watched for a moment as it flickered and settled. Setting it over the bureau between his bed and the next, he finally stretched out and pulled up the thin wool blanket that had been folded neatly at the foot of the bed. "That will wake us up in a couple of hours."

"Amazing," Vyra said. "I'm no stranger to magic, but your skills are something else again."

Tashi yawned and turned on his side. "I was training to be Warlock Prime. My tutor was Master Rumér Vega." He meant to stop there, but couldn't help adding, "You should see what I can do when I'm properly kitted."

"I can't picture you in warlock shine," Ezhil said. "You'd just sell it all, same as the rest of us."

"Go to sleep," Vyra said.

Tashi obeyed, but damned if he didn't smile faintly at the way Ezhil included him in that 'us.'

He fell asleep quickly, but woke up far too soon, his cantrip chiming gently but still somehow far too loud and annoying. Tashi banished it as he sat up and stretched, groaning as he tried to work out the kinks in his back and neck.

A strangled noise came from behind him; he rose and turned to see what was wrong, but found only Vyra bent over his shoes, and Ezhil still in bed, facing the window opposite the door. "Get your lazy ass up."

Ezhil groaned. "I don't wanna. Leave me alone."

"Up or I'll zap you."

"Whatever happened to being seduced out of bed?" Ezhil grumbled as he finally sat up and took his own turn at stretching and groaning, finally shoving the mess that was his hair out of his face. "Fuck me these beds are atrocious. Sleeping on the ground would be better."

Vyra snorted. "Glad you think so, because that's what we'll be doing for the foreseeable future."

"Let's go," Tashi said as he finished dressing, fervently hoping his stupid, horribly impractical shoes would last him until he could acquire a useful pair of boots. "Where are we headed?"

"Western gate," Vyra said. "I admit I don't know how we'll get through it without drawing attention. They must have guards and magic in place to be on the lookout for us."

Tashi and Ezhil laughed. "Leave that to the body takers," Ezhil said.

Leaving the bedroom, Ezhil went back to the storage room, where they grabbed some satchels and knapsacks, which they filled with food and other supplies that could be obtained quickly and easily. Ready, they headed out into a night that proved to be cold and foggy, light and shadows distorted by it.

The last time he'd seen the weather like this was the night he'd been thrown out. Marvelous.

"Don't suppose Your Highness has a cantrip for getting rid of fog?" Ezhil muttered.

"No, and stop calling me that, seriously. Right now it's just going to draw attention we don't need."

"Fine, fine."

Tashi shivered despite himself, not dressed for the unexpected cold snap. He didn't mind chilly, especially as the weather moved on toward spring, but this was significantly colder than that. Suspiciously so. Damn it.

"I thought winter was *ending*," Vyra said. "Maybe we should go back for cloaks."

"No point," Tashi said. "I think this weather is magic-induced, and won't extend past the city. We just need to keep going."

Ezhil gave him a look but didn't speak. He didn't have to. Weather magic was illegal. The only person in the city who could possibly be allowed to cast it was Rumér. If he wasn't doing it, then somebody was doing it unsanctioned.

Tashi genuinely didn't know which

scenario was worse. Hopefully they wouldn't have to find out. He whispered a soft cantrip and cast it over each of them in turn, ensuring that they'd go overlooked should they run into anyone else in this weather. Another cantrip, compatible with the first, softened the noises they made, rendering them even more invisible. "That's all I dare do; anything more and the magic will start to stand out."

After that, they lapsed into silence, communicating with looks and gestures whenever they had to duck out of the way of someone else wandering in the fog. Yes, the magic was there, but the less they had to depend on it, the better.

Normally the walk to the western gate should have taken twenty or so minutes from their starting point, but with the fog and caution, it took them more than an hour. Two hours of sleep had been nowhere near enough for how long this stupid day was going to be.

As they drew close to the gate, Ezhil took over the lead, cutting down an alleyway that came out a block or two south of the gate entrance—and right by one of the many drainage ditches that kept the city from flooding when the river got carried away with itself. They were relatively small, just barely large enough for one person to squeeze through, and blocked with bars, but that sort of challenge never slowed the determined and intrepid down for long.

In this case, all you had to do was swim down deep enough to go *under* the bars, since the city builders had been either too cheap or too lazy or both to extend them all the way down.

"Wait," he said, as Ezhil started to wade into the water. "Something doesn't feel right."

"Doesn't feel right how?" Vyra asked, looking around, tensing for a fight.

Tashi cast his senses out, trying to trace the source of the tingling at the back of his neck, softly replying, "Magic."

Just as he pinged it, the source came out of the shadows that had been hiding it: Rumér, as beautiful and untouchable as ever. "So the fog and cold *are* your doing."

Rumér's smile was as faint as fading mist. "At your sister's request."

"Jana has never requested anything a single day of her life. So what, now you haul me back to the fucking palace? I don't care if you will kick my ass, I'm not going without a fight."

A laugh as faint as Rumér's smile floated around them. "Tashi, if I really wanted to take you in, I'd have laid a trap that even you can't escape, not as you are right now. I just came to say farewell. I'm sorry I dragged you into this mess. I genuinely just wanted your help. I didn't know Her Highness was going to act like this. Wherever you're going, be careful—and take this." He tossed something, and Tashi caught it deftly, noting the weight of the small bag, even as he tucked it away to more closely examine later.

Tashi turned away, mind a tumult, but mostly just a rant about his stupidity and insanity.

Insanity

"Wait!" he said, turning back.

Rumér froze. "What?"

"In the Midden, I completely forgot with the whole being accused of murder thing. I destroyed a Circle of Frenzy. There will be several more all over the city. I never had a chance to find them."

Rumér swore. "I see. Thank you for telling me. I will find and destroy them. I can't believe I never noticed them to begin with."

"Probably tied to whoever is cursing Her Majesty. Do you want—"

"What I want doesn't matter," Rumér said firmly, looking tired and sad for a bare moment. "You need to go, Tashi. Our problems aren't yours anymore. Run while you can. I'm sorry, so sorry, things did not turn out better. Farewell."

Then Rumér was gone, with a finality that hurt.

"Let's get the fuck out of here," Tashi said before the others could ask questions he didn't want to answer.

Ezhil gave him a mocking salute, then turned and dove smoothly into the water. A couple of minutes later came a faint, "Clear!" from the other side of the wall, which wasn't exactly narrow.

"You're next," Tashi said. "Unless you can't swim? Fuck me, we should have thought to ask."

Vyra laughed and offered a toothy smile. "I'm a feral, Your Highness. I can swim just fine."

Tashi groaned. "Don't you start!"

Still laughing, Vyra waded into the water.

Once he too had called he was clear, Tashi drew a deep breath and let it out slowly. He'd left the city before, but only for official trips. There'd always been his retinue, bodyguards, friends and hangers-on. He'd traveled on strict schedules, with little to nothing left to chance, always moving from one secured, tightly regulated location to another. At times it had felt like he'd never really left at all.

He'd slipped out a couple of times when getting rid of a body required it, but moving along the fringes of the wall didn't really count as leaving the city.

This was the first time he'd truly be leaving the city, seeing the rest of the world as it really was, instead of viewing it through the diamond-studded windows of a place he no longer belonged.

Not once had he ever really believed this would happen.

If only he didn't have to come back.

On that dangerous thought, Tashi dove into the water and swam down, down, down into the murky depths, working by feel to find the bars and then going deeper still.

After he was clear, it was a frantic swim up, barely reaching the shore before his lungs gave out on him, the need for air bursting from him as he collapsed on the edge of the bank. "Fuck that swim."

"Agreed," Ezhil replied. "At least this time we weren't hauling bodies."

Tashi gave him a look as he climbed to his feet and cast cantrips for drying and warming over all of them. "Why would a snatcher need to come out here?"

"To haul back in the bodies you fucking catchers let go to waste," Ezhil replied.

"Ugh."

Vyra laughed, casting them an amused look as they headed off together away from the city, into the scraggly woods and rolling hills beyond.

They walked until sunrise, when they were hours out of the city and could rest with relative safety that nobody would be coming after them.

Sitting down with a groan, Tashi removed his shitty shoes and examined his sore, bloody feet, whispering cantrips to heal the worst of the damage. Nearby, Vyra had gotten a fire going, and Ezhil was digging out food. "I'll go find bedding."

"Sit, sit," Vyra said, casting him a brief look. "You're the only one not wearing boots, and we've got a lot of walking to do yet. Want to be useful, do some of your fancy magic. What did that man back in the city give you, speaking of fancy?"

Tashi blinked, then rubbed his eyes. "Oh, right. I'd completely forgotten about that." He reached into his knapsack and pulled out the pouch Rumér had tossed him. It was made from buttery soft brown leather, lined with what looked like dark blue velvet, enchanted to resist water and other damage.

Shrugging out of his jacket, Tashi smoothed it across his lap, then opened the pouch and dumped out the contents.

Glittering jewels flashed at him in the sunlight, along with gleaming gold and silver. There was also a small cloth bundle, rolled tightly and secured with ribbon. He picked it up and undid the ribbon, tucking that away in a pocket. Unrolling the fabric, which proved to be two pieces, he smoothed them out to reveal gloves, an old ache throbbing in his chest.

They were thin, woven of delicate but sturdy mage silk, open at the fingertips, fitted precisely to his hands. Well, they had been once. He doubted they'd fit all that well anymore, but maybe…

Pulling them on took some doing, as the fit really was meant to be second skin, but at last he was able to button them in place before running his thumb over the buttons themselves. Three of them, carved from bone, shaped to look like sun, moon, and star. The silk itself was deepest blue, almost black, and shimmered faintly here and there where the light caught it.

"Wow," Ezhil said with a whistle. "I don't know what's so special about a pair of fucking gloves, but you look like someone just gave you an engagement ring and a good plowing."

"Shut up," Tashi said without any heat. "They're cantrip gloves; meant to protect the hands of the user from the collateral damage some rings can cause, since rings tend to be the most powerful talismans we use." He'd always been inordinately fond of his, enjoying the way they felt, wrapped so close, soft against his skin, making his hands look finer and prettier than they really were.

He'd thought he'd managed to get rid of all his stupid vanity, but he supposed some of it was always going to linger.

Ignoring the stares he could still feel, Tashi turned his attention to the jewelry. Rumér had handed over a good third of Tashi's once-prized collection. None of the really dangerous stuff, the rings and bracelets and pendants that would most certainly draw attention, but all of it useful and nothing to scoff at.

Unfortunately, much would still draw unwanted attention, so those pieces he tucked away again, to be brought out only when circumstances left him no choice.

Of the remaining were five rings, two ear cuffs, a bracelet, and a silver necklace from which dangled a small black opal. That he went ahead and fastened in place. The chain was short, meaning it was snug around his throat.

Next, he sorted through the rings, finally decided on three, tucking the remaining two back into the leather bag. After some consideration, he tucked the bracelet away as well. Leaving only the cuffs. One was gold, shaped to look like a little dragon was perched on his ear; the other was silver, shaped to look like twining vines scattered with jeweled flowers.

Tashi took down his messy hair, combed it out with his fingers as best he could, then braided it deftly back, securing the end with the ribbon he'd tucked away before. Once that was done, he presented the cuffs to his companions, who were watching him avidly, because apparently watching a man put on jewelry was a novelty. "Gold or silver?"

"Silver," Ezhil and Vyra said together, an odd tone to their voices.

Giving them a look, Tashi tucked the gold one away and closed the bag before curling the silver cuff into place. Shoving the bag into his satchel, he yawned and pulled his jacket back on.

He paused to look over and feel his jewelry, heart racing. He really had missed his warlock shine, stupid as that was. He felt settled now in a way he never had before, not even back when he'd still been a prince. Like he was right where he should, exactly as he should be.

Chapter Eleven

Shaking the strange feeling off, he dropped his hands and turned to the other, drawing up short to see they were staring at him again. "What?"

"So, uh, what exactly does all that stuff do?" Vyra asked. "I don't really know anything about magic, not at that level."

Tashi replied, "Jewels are power. Strictly speaking, power is all around us—in every leaf, every blade of grass, even the air we breathe. We can't access that power, though, not easily. We can only draw upon our own power, and sometimes anything near us that resonates strongly enough, though that's exceedingly rare. Jewels, though…they're like sponges for power. Different jewels absorb power from different things, work best for different kinds of magic. The larger the jewel, the greater its clarity, the more power it can contain."

"Doesn't the royal family have some giant diamond or something?" Ezhil asked. "Hear stories about it all the time. Big as a head, some say big a person."

"The quartz is that big," Tashi said with a laugh. "There's a gigantic piece of purple quartz in the private hall of the royal wing, where my family lives. It's largely decorative though; quartz doesn't hold power very well. It serves as basically fuel for the lights on that hall, that's about it. There *is* a large blue diamond in the vault, and it 's even more powerful than you can imagine, but it's an emergency supply, to be used only under direst circumstances, like the city under siege. If a warlock was to use all that power too quickly, the overload would kill them. They keep it under heavy lock and key. Only my mother has access. The rest of the jewels in the vault are vastly more interesting. These—" he waved to the jewels he was wearing "—are the barest hint of my collection, and I would have been given still more once I was officially Warlock Prime."

"This is going to sound like a stupid question, probably…" Ezhil said, then faltered.

Tashi gave him a look. "I have never known you to miss an opportunity to say or do something stupid."

"Fuck you, Tashi," Ezhil retorted. "You have *no room* to talk on that matter. I'm not the one who used to be royalty and probably could be again if I'd just stop being a fucking baby."

"Just ask your damned question."

"Exactly how powerful are you really?"

That wasn't the question Tashi had been expecting. "Back when I was a prince, with no assistance whatsoever? Better than average, less than great. With my jewels? I would have been the best in the queendom, except for Rumér, who has significant experience on me." Given time and experience, he would have surpassed Rumér. Tashi had been born for magic, and it would always leave him aching that he'd lost his chance to be great at it. "Now I'm just Tashi? Average at best on my own, good with my jewels. Any more questions?"

Ezhil opened his mouth, but closed it again at a look from Vyra. "Right, we're supposed to be working, not gawking at the pretty royal warlock in all his sparkly glory and asking questions."

Tashi let out a long sigh. "The minute we come to a river, I'm throwing you in it."

"Yeah, yeah. I'm going to gather what we need for bedding."

"I'll deal with food," Vyra said, mouth quirking. "I sense I'm the only one who can."

Tashi laughed. "You're not wrong."

"Using a campfire can't be any harder than

using a stove," Ezhil said, scoffing.

Vyra just laughed, and Ezhil made a face at him before walking off into the woods.

Tashi was more than happy to remove his lousy shoes and settle more comfortably in front of the fire. After their swim in the rank waters of the Oss and trekking about soaking wet, the warmth of the fire almost made him groan.

Silence stretched on, peaceful and soothing, for several minutes. Tashi drifted between dozing lightly and watching Vyra work—and nearly jumped out of his skin when Vyra spoke.

"If everything wasn't such a mess, with your sister and everything… if all was wiped clean, past and present… would you go back?" Vyra asked. "It must be hard to go from being a prince to being a body catcher."

Tashi's mouth flattened, and he stared down at his hands, covered in mage silk for the first time in more than a decade. It wasn't the body catching that had nearly broken him. It was the whoring. Going from being important to being nothing at all. "No, I wouldn't. That probably sounds utterly stupid and spoiled, but… that world is full of *real* rot. I was a spoiled brat. I knew what I was, what I was going to be, and I gloried in it. Modesty? For the weak. Humility? For fools. Kindness? Only when it suited my purposes or my mood. No one was more shocked than me when I for once in my life stepped up and did the right thing—but that right thing was murder, even if I didn't do it on purpose, and my mother handled the problem. Whether she handled it correctly or not is irrelevant at this point."

"Sounds like your mother *made* the problem. I've seen the type. Don't see why you shouldn't go back, though, given how much better you've become. I can't see you as you've described. I think the person you've become would do well as a prince."

"Maybe, but I doubt it," Tashi said. "Even if I could be assured of that… I'd prefer a middle ground. Something better than the Rotter, something less poisonous than royal prince. Something…" That would let him use magic again—use it in ways that *mattered.*

"Something…?"

"Nothing that matters," Tashi replied. "What about you, Vyra? What did you leave behind to come save your sister? Will she be all right without you?"

"She'll be fine, and I'll write her a letter when we reach our destination. I was never anything special. My family isn't poor, not by Ossiri standards, but we're not exactly well to do, either. Back home I was a city sweeper. Here I shovel shit. Not much difference between the jobs, honestly. People are messy, and someone always has to clean up the messes. I wish I could do better for my sister. She did not have a pleasant upbringing, being a woman who not only had opinions but voiced them. Ossiri is good for her in that respect, but I wish I could do better than a falling down house in the Midden." He shrugged. "We'll see where I stand when all this is over."

Tashi bit his tongue on pointing out that for Vyra, it *could* be over. He could take his contraband coins, Night he could take Tashi's share too, and go back to Ossiri and never worry about this mess ever again. Nobody in the Midden would give him up, and he wouldn't know a damn thing about what Tashi got up to beyond the city.

Selfishly, he didn't want Vyra to go, though. Not yet. So instead he only said, "Shit, does that mean Ezhil is the only one among us with a normal family and upbringing?"

"Wouldn't go that far, given my mother gambled everything away," Ezhil said as he rejoined them, lugging a ridiculously large pile of leafy branches, red-faced and panting. "Hang on." He vanished again briefly, returning with more branches. Vyra waved him to sit down and took over setting up the beds while Ezhil and Tashi watched their dinner bubble away. "My mother the gambler, my father the useless pile who left us instead of dealing with any of the problems he married. No idea where he is now." He shrugged. "Close to my other relatives, though, who've been kind enough to not blame me for the failings of my parents. They're normal enough, I guess."

"Why didn't they help when you had to

turn whore, they're so normal? What about your ex-wife, when she was still your wife?"

"The short answer is that it's complicated," Ezhil replied. "The less short answer is that they'd already helped my mother a thousand times, I didn't want to ask them for more help. By the time they knew about it, I was already a body snatcher. They pester me from time to time to work in the restaurant instead, but I like the freedom body snatching affords, whatever its risks. I'll spare you the long answer. As to my ex-wife, we were very young, very infatuated, very stupid. We finally admitted that, divorced, and happily went our separate ways." He poured himself some of the tea that Vyra had set brewing. "So when are you going to tell us where we're going?"

"It wasn't a secret or anything." Vyra finished the bed piles and resumed his seat, stirring the simmering porridge he had going. "We're headed for a feral encampment in No Man's Land."

Tashi gave him a look, one brow lifting. "Don't think they're gonna be thrilled about human guests."

"You're my guests, and I have enough clout they'll allow it, so long as you two behave. I know that's asking a lot, but try."

Tashi and Ezhil laughed, and Ezhil said, "I promise nothing. He always starts it, anyway, so keep an eye on him."

Tashi rolled his eyes. Standing, he put his

satchel at one end of his bed to make a pillow. Thankfully, the weather was much nicer out here than it had been in the city, so he'd be fine sleeping without a cloak, even if he always felt better when something was covering him. "When will food be ready?"

"Not for a time, yet," Vyra replied. "I'm making a lot, so I can turn some of it into cakes. Save us time cooking further on. Go ahead and sleep if you want. We'll have to take turns on watch, anyway, you can eat when your turn comes up. Porridge will be overcooked by then, but still plenty edible."

"I've eaten way worse than overdone porridge. Thank you, I appreciate it." Yawning, he stretched out on his bed, shuffling until the most stabbing bits of branch were no longer bothering him. They really would need to acquire cloaks eventually, if only to make travel slightly less miserable.

Closing his eyes, Tashi focused on his breathing, on relaxing enough to fall asleep. Eventually, though, it was the soft lull of his friends conversing that finally let him drift away.

~~*

He woke to someone shaking his shoulder, and groaned into his makeshift pillow. "Lemme alone."

"Get up, pretty boy," Ezhil said cheerfully.

Tashi groaned again, then pushed himself upright. "Up, I'm up. I have a name you know, you could try using it."

"Why would I use your name when it's so much more fun to call you 'Your Highness' and 'pretty boy'?" Ezhil said, then yawned. "Wake us around dawn."

Tashi gave a lazy salute and stood as Ezhil headed over to his own bed. He shuffled into the woods to relieve himself, then ambled back to the fire and fixed a bowl of porridge. Overcooked as expected, but warm and filling, so he had no complaints.

Vyra snored softly on his pallet, and Ezhil was already fast asleep on his. Tashi looked up at the stars, which hadn't changed at all, but were certainly clearer and brighter without the interference of the city.

He marked the constellations from habit. The Huntress. The Shadow. The Great River. The Blood River. The Basket. The Rabbits. The Snake. Crown of Night. The Scepter. The Warlock. He'd spent many a night on the roof of the palace studying the stars with Rumér. If only he'd appreciated those times more. Had understood then just how easily such things could be ripped away.

Finishing his porridge, he set the bowl aside to clean once it was light out and idly looked over his companions again. Friends. Even Ezhil. After all the three of them had been through lately, how could he call them anything else? He was amazed they were still with him, instead of running as far and fast as they could, leaving him in the dust. That would be the smart thing to do. They were only in trouble because of him. If they weren't around him anymore…

He still wasn't in a hurry to remind them of that, though, however foolish that made him. Hadn't he learned all these years that keeping to himself was the best policy? It was getting mixed up with other people—first Dawa, then Rumér— that had brought all this damned trouble down on his head.

When everything was over, he'd have to do something especially nice to say thanks. What that was, he didn't know. *Nice* wasn't exactly in his skillset. The most he did was show some respect when disposing of a body, no matter how much of a cretin they'd been in real life.

With nothing else to do while he watched for hungry animals and uninvited strangers, Tashi turned his attention to what he loved best: magic.

His jewelry thrummed to life as he called up his power, tingling along his skin and sparking in his blood. As a body catcher, he tended to use the same handful of cantrips, and rarely had there been reason to use magic otherwise, save the protection cantrips for his flat.

So he went back to the basics, starting with the most trivial training exercise, the one every student learned second. The first was a minor cage, more often called a bubble, in which he could cast the cantrips so that they were rendered effectively harmless. Everything happened within the bubble, reacting if cast correctly, doing nothing if cast incorrectly. Most students were not allowed to use magic outside of the bubble for at least three months. Tashi had been ready after barely one.

Kal. Tal. Ral. Pal. Sal. Mal. Aal. Bal. Fal. Dal.
Kel. Tel. Rel. Pel. Sel. Mel. Ael. Bel. Fel. Del.
Kol. Tol. Rol. Pol. Sol. Mol. Aol. Bol. Fol. Dol.
Kil. Til. Ril. Pil. Sil. Mil. Ail. Bil. Fil. Dil.
Kul. Tul. Rul. Pul. Sul. Mul. Aul. Bul. Ful.
Dul.

The fifty foundation cantrips. From them all other cantrips were formed. In training, it was called Center. Next came the First Ring.

Kel-aal-sol. Fire.
Kel-aal-dol. Water.
Kel-aal-rol. Earth
Kel-aal-tol. Wind.

Tashi pushed onward, going through the First, Second, and Third Rings before he finally called a halt. The point was to practice, warm up, not exhaust himself. Dismissing the bubble, Tashi put the kettle, thankfully full, over the fire and located a mug and what looked like a tin of tea. Prying the lid off, he sniffed—yes, tea. Green, not black, but he was hardly picky.

When he'd finished the tea, he had another

bowl of porridge, and then returned to practicing.

He'd just finished the Center and was beginning the First Ring when a groggy voice said, "What are you doing?"

"Practicing," Tashi said, stopping and banishing the bubble. "It's been a long time since I've needed my magic for more than making my life easier. Much like the guards have their training, so do I. Go back to sleep."

"Need to piss." So saying, Ezhil pushed to his feet and shuffled off into the trees.

When he returned a short time later, he sat on his pallet instead of lying down again. "Can I ask a question?"

"I would be astonished if you didn't," Tashi said with a soft laugh, mindful that Vyra was still asleep. "Is this the one you tried to ask earlier?"

"Yeah. Something has been bugging me ever since you talked about how good you are at magic."

Tashi frowned. "What do you mean?"

"If you're the second best in the country, and I suspect were gonna be *the* best one day… why would your mother throw such great skill away over one murder? Because I'm not stupid. What's more, my line of work lets me see more than uppities think I see. They kill people, accidentally and otherwise, all the fucking time. One murder, and only by accident, by the queen's only son wasn't enough to toss you—especially not with that kind of skill. So why did she really throw you out?"

Tashi opened his mouth. Closed it. His heart pounded, echoing in his chest and head like clanging bells.

Ezhil's eyes widened. "Oh, Night. You never—"

"No," Tashi said, voice cracking roughly. "I never thought to ask that question. I don't know. All these years..."

"I'm sorry," Ezhil said, voice barely above a whisper, eyes still wide. "I'm so sorry. I just assumed..."

Tashi gave a shaky, bitter laugh. "I mean, that definitely should have occurred to me at some point over the years. I just took it at face value: killed somebody, got thrown out instead of executed out of some warped motherly pity." The question, the realization, churned in his stomach.

Why had his mother really gotten rid of him?

In the next breath, though, came a more relevant question: what in the Night did it matter now? Whatever her plotting, she'd succeeded. Now she was dying, unless Rumér or his worthless sister managed to save her.

"I'm sorry," Ezhil said again.

"Shut up and go back to sleep, you ass end of a goat," Tashi said. "Who cares why my mother threw me out? I certainly don't. Now let me practice in peace."

"Tashi..." Ezhil didn't finish whatever he'd

been about to say, only sighed and lay down, and moments later was asleep again.

Tashi resumed practice, until he could no longer focus well. Fixing a last cup of tea, he sipped as he settled into a lull, not dozing, not entirely awake, listening to everything around him and letting his mind simply be.

As the sky turned from solid black to deep gray, and the stars faded from sight, he weighed his options. Ezhil had said to wake them 'around dawn,' but that could mean now or once the sun was up. They needed to be moving, but Vyra and Ezhil could also use the extra sleep, as there was no telling how much sleep they'd be getting between here and their final destination.

So Tashi let them sleep. As far as they'd traveled before stopping for the night, it was highly unlikely anyone from the city would find them, and any beasts in the woods surely would have found them by now.

He considered trying to make breakfast, but even pretending he knew what that entailed, he'd likely burn them and the forest down trying. He also didn't trust himself not to get lost trying to forage something for breakfast. So he settled for keeping the fire going and making a fresh pot of tea, which was easy enough.

Next he bundled up his own meagre belongings so they were ready to go. After that, there was literally nothing left to do, though, and the sky was swiftly turning from gray to purple.

Time to wake up his companions, then.

Just as he stood to do so, however, the woods filled with the sound of something crashing through the trees. Well, fuck. Hopefully it was nothing ba—

A booming roar cut through the morning, sending birds and smaller animals fleeing for their lives.

Chapter Twelve

"So much for that," Tashi muttered. Looked like it was going to be an absolutely *splendid* morning. Maybe they'd get lucky and whatever it was would go somewhere else, not come crashing into their campsite. If only it was people. Those he could deal with. A wild animal big enough to make that much noise? Not so much.

"What the fuck!" Ezhil said as a second roar sounded, louder and closer than ever.

Vyra groaned and grunted, sitting up slowly. "What's all the ruckus—" He stopped as the roar came a third time. "Well. Fuck. We need to get high. *Now.*"

Tashi didn't bother to ask why or if he was sure, just bolted for the nearest tree and scaled it as quickly as he possibly could, pausing only to ensure the other two had found trees as well. Certain of that, he resumed climbing, going as high as he dared.

He made it to a wide, sturdy branch, with a smaller, closer one he could cling to, just in time.

The crashing sound, and that awful roaring, proved to have been made by a tuskbear, an unholy abomination that looked like the unwanted bastard child of a wild boar and a humpback bear. It was enormous, even larger than the bear it resembled, with short, bristly, black-brown fur that would hurt if rubbed the wrong way. It had enormous hooves that could tear up hardened earth like it was soft mud, four long, wickedly curved tusks jutting from a mouth filled with razor sharp teeth meant for tearing and shredding, and if that wasn't enough, at the back of every foot was a hooked claw. The fucking bastard had more sharp bits than any one creature needed, surely.

Speaking of sharp bits, there was also a sword sticking out of its back. Somebody had already tried to kill the bastard once, and clearly had not succeeded, may they rest in peace.

Tashi had only ever seen them in books, and as heads mounted on walls, and he fervently wished that was still true.

The fucking thing rooted around the campsite, clearly looking for an easy meal. Tashi ran through everything he knew about them.

Tuskbears were stubbornly resistant to magic, save for fire, which to be fair, would fuck up anyone's day.

Unfortunately, the jewelry piece that would have provided him with plenty of fire magic was in his jewelry bag, because he'd gone with the silver one. Probably for the best, though, given fire tended to have a mind of its own, and they were in the middle of a forest. Killing a tuskbear by starting a forest fire was the exact opposite of solving the problem.

On that note, he should probably put out their fire before something tragic happened. Calling up a cantrip for water, he drew it quickly and threw it at the fire, releasing the breath he'd been holding when it worked and the fire went out.

Unfortunately, the magic and movement drew the tuskbear's attention right to him, and with another of those awful roars, the bastard ran headlong into Tashi's tree. If he hadn't been braced for it, he'd have fallen right out of it and onto the waiting tusks.

"Fuck you," Tashi muttered. Clinging for dear life to the branch with one arm, he used his free hand to draw a cantrip on the trunk of the tree, then pressed his hand against it to activate. The cantrip turned into light and poured down the trunk, bringing up black-green vines from which long, nasty, red-tipped thorns burst.

The tuskbear slammed into the trunk, and

Tashi fed more energy into the spell, ignoring the vertigo of too much magic too fast combined with being shaken like a nut tree.

As the tuskbear screamed in pain, stuck on the thorns puncturing its entire face, Tashi switched his focus to the vines, sweat beading on his brow and dripping down his face like tears as he coaxed the vines to wrap and wrap and wrap, until the tuskbear collapsed from exhaustion and pain.

Then he tightened them, and after a few minutes the tuskbear finally died from lack of air.

"Fuck," he said, wiping the sweat from his face. "Someone else gets the next one."

Ezhil dropped from his tree and drew his knife. "I've never seen magic like that. Nicely done, Your Highness."

Tashi heaved a sigh and then set to climbing carefully down his own tree, not stupid enough to attempt Ezhil's flashy decent. "Well, it was that or we learned how to make boar hunting spears real fucking fast."

Vyra laughed as he landed smoothly from his own jump. Apparently everyone was a showoff *except* the warlock.

Landing with far less elegance than the other two, Tashi huffed and said, "So now what do we do with the stupid thing?"

"Are you certain it's dead?"

"It's dead," Vyra said. "Trust me, we'd know if it wasn't."

Ezhil eyed the vine-wrapped tuskbear warily. "Could be passed out."

"You'd see it breathing," Vyra replied, and pulled out his knife. Going over to the tuskbear, he cut away several vines until he found whatever he was looking for, and then, judging by location and movement, slit the tuskbear's throat.

Hot blood went everywhere, and Vyra backed away from the mess with a grimace. "At least it only seems to have gotten my pants and boots. Should have stood to the side. Oh, well. If we stay here a little longer, or at least don't go far, I can butcher this thing and smoke the meat, give us plenty to eat while we travel and more than enough to barter with later."

"May as well stay here," Tashi said. "I'll set up wards, if someone will come with me to keep me from getting lost in this damned place."

Ezhil laughed. "Guess that's me, since Vyra is doing the butchering. Be back in a bit if you need my help, Vyra."

Vyra lifted a hand to acknowledge the words, but didn't reply otherwise, focused on his work.

"Where do you want to set up these wards of yours?" Ezhil asked.

"At one hundred and two hundred paces, roughly, from the campsite, in a full circle. That should give us plenty of warning, both of arrival and then how quickly they're approaching. More than enough time to grab essentials and bolt. I can try to go out to five hundred paces, but that would take all day, at best, and deplete me."

"I think one and two is more than enough," Ezhil said. "Assuming it's royal soldiers or the like coming after us, they make more noise than our new dinner." He threw Tashi a grin. "Not unlike Your Highness trying to get in and out of a tree."

"Oh, shut up," Tashi said. "Let's not forget that you're only here because you needed my help getting out of a fight with the city guards and then escaping a prison wagon."

"All of that is your fault, so don't go judging me," Ezhil replied, still grinning. "Here, a hundred paces. I can't guarantee I can lead us in a perfect circle, but I'll come reasonably close."

"Thanks." Tashi drew the warding cantrips in the air, a dual drawing that used his first and last fingers, making the warding look like one color was a shadow of the other. It hung there in the air as he finished, waiting for the completion of the chain before it would fully set. "Next point, about twenty, twenty-five paces from this one. How do you not get lost? It all looks the same."

"I've always had a good sense of direction and wandering around here isn't any harder than navigating the sewers—and a good deal more pleasant."

"I don't want to think that anything could be worse."

Ezhil laughed again, and fuck but Tashi was starting to enjoy way too much how often he got Ezhil to do that. Real laughter, not all their posturing and taunting. If he didn't watch himself, he'd start thinking of how nice it would be to do something even stupider, like kiss the infuriating bastard.

Uuuggghhh. No, that was officially the last time he had such a stupid thought.

Thankfully, setting the wards and avoiding not tripping over something took the bulk of his attention, and Ezhil's idle chatter occupied the rest of it. By the time they were finally finished, Tashi was ready to go right back to sleep. He would cheerfully kill for a comfortable bed, but it had been so long since he'd slept in one of those, he wasn't sure he actually remembered how it felt.

Back at camp, there were now three fires going, and a truly impressive amount of smoke. There was also enough meat to feed approximately two hundred people, and Vyra looked even more ready for a nap than Tashi.

"You two rest before you fall over," Ezhil said. "I know a thing or two about preparing food: I can keep an eye on this. You two won't be of any use if we get attacked or have to run. Found some mushrooms and a few other things while we were out putting up His Highness's wards. Dinner tonight shouldn't be too bad at all."

"Are you sure?" Tashi asked, even as a yawn got the better of him. "Nevermind. I'm going to sleep. Standing watch and killing nightmares and setting wards has wrung me out."

So saying, he sprawled on his bedroll, tucked his pack under his head for a pillow, and closed his eyes. The heat from the trio of fires was almost too hot, but it was leagues better than being cold. Anything was better than being cold, and the only thing worse was being cold and wet.

Tashi turned his mind to other things before bad memories could get hold of him.

It was entirely too easy to drift to sleep on thoughts of Ezhil and Vyra, the only people he had felt like calling friends in more years than he cared to think about. To fall asleep listening to their voices, more soothing than the lullabies his nurse had sung to him as a child.

He woke to their voices as well, and the crackle-snap of a single fire. Despite the uncomfortable bed, he was warm and comfy enough he didn't want to move, didn't even want to open his eyes. As silence fell, though, concern took comfort's place, and he dragged his eyes open to make certain nothing bad had happened in the few seconds he'd been awake.

What greeted his eyes was almost worse.

Across the fire, Ezhil and Vyra were kissing. Softly, more exploratory than amorous, but a kiss all the same. It felt like someone had punched Tashi in the face.

That was stupid, though, the melodramatic, entitled behavior of a spoiled prince. He had claim on neither of them. Mere days ago he and Ezhil hadn't even *liked* each other.

Why should he care if they wanted to—

He couldn't even finish the thought.

Tashi closed his eyes again, stomach churning. Why couldn't he have just stayed asleep a little longer? He'd settle for going back to sleep, but he needed to piss too badly for that. So instead he closed his eyes, then made a noisier production about waking up before heaving to his feet and stumbling off to piss.

When he returned, Vyra was tending to the tuskboar meat and Ezhil was making more tea. The world might very well collapse if they ever ran out of tea. "Did I miss anything exciting?"

"No, thankfully, though it was close," Vyra said. "We heard another one of these nightmares, but I think the stench of one of its own being roasted spooked it off."

"I really can't wait to be out of this fucking forest," Tashi said, sitting by the fire to warm his hands.

How precisely did one go about asking his friends about a kiss he wasn't meant to have seen? One didn't, he supposed. It was their choice to tell him or not. He wished they'd go ahead and get it over with.

Funny that Vyra kept teasing him and Ezhil for sounding like an old married couple, and Ezhil had insisted Vyra had been giving him 'fuck me' eyes. They'd been fighting for their lives, though. Where in the Night in that mess was he supposed to have realized how he felt, let alone acted on it?

Clearly he should have figured it out. Then again, if they were kissing each other…

Ugh, he was tired of the whole fucking mess. He didn't need this. They could do whatever they wanted. "So when do we leave? Are we staying through the night?"

"We were hoping once you were awake we could pack up and head out, travel until it grows dark and maybe even try to keep going." Ezhil shrugged. "That would rely entirely on you, though, so we weren't sure."

"Me? Oh, to light our way." Tashi smiled, despite still fervently wishing he was asleep. Or dead. "I can provide light—that's a parlor trick. Not getting lost or going in circles, that's the hard part, and I'm useless for that. All these stupid trees look the same."

"I can guide us, if you can light the way," Vyra said with a smile of his own.

Tashi wouldn't mind learning how that smile tasted, but it was too fucking late for that, wasn't it?

"Are you all right?" Vyra asked. "You seem… upset."

"Fine. Just still groggy, I guess. Is there food?"

"Freshly smoked tuskbear, ready and waiting," Ezhil said, tossing a small packet to Tashi. "Enjoy." His eyes were far more pensive and knowing, and if Tashi didn't know any better, he'd swear the bastard was quietly smirking.

"Let's get going then, shall we?" He unwrapped the packet, which proved to be made of leaves, and tore off a chunk of meat. "This is really good."

Vyra smiled. "Should see what I can do with a fully stocked kitchen."

They broke down camp, made certain the fire was well and truly out, and headed off. Tashi disbanded the wards as they passed them, then focused on not tripping over things and eating his food.

With hours of daylight ahead of them, they made good time, especially with the ease and confidence Vyra led with, as though he knew the forest like his own face.

As dusk began to fall, Tashi cast lights for them to see by—at each of their shoulders, along the ground, and well ahead to warn off anything that might prove to be a problem. "I can't wait to never have to hike through the woods again."

Ezhil snickered. "Poor prince, with not a carriage and twenty servants in sight."

Tashi scoffed. "I traveled with ten servants, *thank you*."

That made them laugh, and Tashi smiled despite himself. Maybe nobody wanted to kiss him, but they were still his friends, even with all the drama that had come rushing back into his life.

"What's this, then?" Ezhil asked, drawing

Tashi from his thoughts.

He stared at the fork in the crude path they'd been following, then up at the signpost just a few paces in front of him. Unfortunately, no one had spelled it against the elements, or they'd done so poorly, because the words were long faded and the sign on the verge of collapsing entirely. "I can tell you right now that if someone so much as says the word 'shortcut,' I'm leaving you right here and taking the longest route possible."

Ezhil snorted a laugh, and Vyra rolled his eyes. Gesturing to the signs, he said, "The paths are roughly the same distance. I suppose one might be shorter than the other, but I don't know for certain, and the difference would be irrelevant. One goes through the foothills then curves north, where you have to then cross a canyon. The other path skips the foothills but requires going through some open, windy valleys where we wouldn't have cover. I believe the foothill path will have an old hunter's cabin we can use, but the valleys will be an easier walk. Those are the only significant differences. They meet up again on the road we need to reach the encampment."

Tashi frowned as they both looked at him. "What?"

"Which way?"

"Why do I have to choose?"

"Because," Ezhil said, folding his arms across his chest and smirking. "Just do as your told, Your Highness."

Tashi rolled his eyes.

"Foothills, then. I don't like the idea of wide, open valleys with no cover, even if we have to do some harder walking."

Ezhil grimaced. "Agreed. I'm used to the city, with buildings everywhere. Being somewhere with no cover at all gives me the creeps."

Vyra chuckled. "You're going to have a lot of adjusting to do at the encampment, then, but I agree the foothills sound better. Especially since that route means we can sleep inside tonight if we make good time." Vyra gave them both a tiny playful shove, and the trio headed off.

Chapter Thirteen

Eventually, Tashi gave up on his stupid, useless shoes entirely, taking them off and walking in just his stockings. His feet wouldn't thank him for it, but they'd have fewer blisters at the end of the day. "There had better be a bed at the end of this journey."

"There was a bed my last trip through, but that was some time ago," Vyra replied. "Still, everyone who travels this way values that cabin. We all leave food and other supplies as we're able. I tend to chop wood when I can afford to stay a few additional hours. There's blankets, food, spare travel supplies, someone even left an old bathing tub."

Tashi might have whimpered. They'd had

marvelous baths back in the house they'd borrowed for a night, but that already felt like ages ago, and his feet would deeply appreciate a hot soak by the time they stopped for the night. "What I wouldn't give for an enormous porcelain tub, steaming water, bath salts, jasmine scented soap and bath oil…"

"What in the world is *bath oil*?" Ezhil asked.

"Scented oils you add to bath water for relaxation and to improve the skin," Tashi said. "Not that there's any saving my skin these days, but I do miss smelling nice."

"You hardly smell terrible," Ezhil retorted, then flushed and looked away.

Tashi had no idea what to make of that, so only replied, "Not that any of us could tell, not after years in the Rotter. Not to mention that last dip before we finally got out of that damn city. But thanks all the same."

"You do smell nice, though." Vyra frowned at him, head tilting. "Like flowers, ever so faintly. What kind of soap do you use?"

"Whatever was in the scrap basket that I can get for a col." Which was definitely never anything scented.

He definitely wasn't going to admit that he stored his soap in scavenged flower petals. He hadn't thought the effect was noticeable to anyone except him, but apparently the stupid trick worked better than he'd always thought.

"Liar, liar, Your Highness," Ezhil said. "You

do often smell like flowers."

"Maybe you're both addled."

Vyra snorted. "Keep your flowery secrets then."

"Oh, for Night's sake!" Tashi threw up his hands. "I steal flowers from the bins of that shop on Silveren Avenue whenever I happen to be in that part of town. I strip the petals, throw them in an old pot I scavenged from a porcelain shop, and store my soap in it. Nothing exciting. I smell like old, thrown out flowers. Well, used to. Now I think I smell like Ossiri and entirely too much fucking walking in a stupid forest."

"I think it's just called sweat," Vyra drawled.

Tashi groaned. "That's it, stop talking to Ezhil; he's a bad influence."

Ezhil snickered, but before he could reply, there was a rustling in the woods ahead—and then seven men, none of them small or slight in build, were blocking the road.

"Oh, for Night's sake," Tashi said again as they came to a stop several paces away. "You have got to be kidding me. Do we look like we have anything worth stealing? My shoes are so shitty I'm carrying them, come on."

The man dead center of the row laughed. "You have plenty of shine on you, warlock. Hand it over."

"No," Tashi retorted, and threw out a hand, channeling his magic into blinding light. "Run!"

Vyra bolted right, into the woods, Ezhil going after him. Tashi cast yet another light spell to buy them a bit more time then ran after his friends, ignoring the shouting and bellowing that came far too close behind them.

He ran until he simply couldn't anymore, the stitch in his side like a knife, and his feet shredded and bloody, his stockings so tattered he may as well be wearing nothing. "Stop, please," he said, and collapsed to his knees, then sat down hard on his ass. His feet were on fire, the pain climbing up his legs where already overworked muscles had worked even harder.

"Fuck," Ezhil said, dropping down in front of him. "You should have said something sooner, you stupid ass ponce."

"Fuck you," Tashi wheezed.

"The cabin isn't too far at this point," Vyra said, and before Tashi could draw a breath to comment, he scooped Tashi up in his arms and resumed moving—thankfully walking now.

Tashi hated it. *Hated* it. Even when his mother had first thrown him on the fucking streets, when he'd learned to sleep in alleys and pick food from garbage bins and whore himself out, he hadn't needed anyone to carry him around.

What was he supposed to do, though? Insist Vyra put him down because he could walk just fine on his own? He couldn't walk at all, let alone *just fine*. With every minute his feet hurt more and more, hot and stinging and stabbing. There was probably all kinds of detritus stuck in the wounds.

Once they could safely stop, he could heal them, at least sufficiently, as he had the night before. "Please tell me they've given up the chase."

Ezhil looked over his shoulder, mouth and brow drawn down as he turned back. "Seem to have, but I'll feel better when we're behind a locked door. I don't understand why they decided to mess with us when they knew full well you were a fucking warlock."

Tashi laughed. "Maybe they figured a warlock who couldn't even afford proper shoes wasn't worth the shine he wore."

"Nice trick with the light," Vyra said. "Smarter than trying to take them on."

"Contrary to the old bard tales, running is generally smarter than fighting," Tashi replied, and started to say more, only to be overtaken by a yawn. Suddenly too tired to keep talking, he let his head fall to rest on Vyra's shoulder.

Not even under pain of death would he ever admit it was nice to be carried, but there was no denying that it was in fact very, *very* nice. Be even better if they weren't wandering a stupid forest and his feet felt like someone had crammed them full of nails and then dunked them in fire.

He didn't stir again until they came to a stop, and only then just enough to take in a cabin that wasn't nearly as ramshackle as he'd been expecting. It was, in fact, rather impressively sturdy, and bigger than he'd anticipated of something called a hunting cabin.

Voices spoke around him, but his eyes were too heavy to open, his head too heavy to lift. All Tashi wanted to do was sleep.

"—down. I'll go—water—"

"Take—food and start—"

Something was wrong. Tashi could hear the urgency in their voices, but his thoughts slipped away before he could sort out what was going on. Sleep, all he wanted was to sleep…

When he woke, it was to the soft murmur of voices, and the sight of Ezhil and Vyra sitting close together in front of a roaring fireplace. The smell of wood and crackling fire, something fragrant that made his stomach growl. "Where…" he broke off, voice hoarse.

The other two snapped around, relief filling their faces. "You're finally awake." Ezhil rose and crossed to him, hastily setting aside a cup that smelled of some flowery tea. "How are you feeling?"

"Sore. Groggy. What happened?"

"You caught a pretty bad fever, some sort of rash. You must have walked in something your body didn't like. Thankfully the cabin is even better supplied than Vyra said, because we were able to get you all fixed up. You've been sleeping most of the night, but the rash is already practically gone. Food is ready if you want some?"

"I want up," Tashi said, voice still raspy. "Something to drink."

Vyra came up already holding a steaming mug. "Fairywort tea, good for healing and strength. I'm so sorry this happened to you, Tashi."

"It's fine. All right, it's not," he added at their expressions, "but it could be a hell of a lot worse than this. So we're at the hunter cabin, I assume?"

"Yes, and just in time, too. Not an hour after we got here it started raining something fierce." Ezhil helped him sit up, and Vyra handed over the cup of tea. "You really like to run your mouth when you're delirious with fever."

Tashi glared. "Thanks, giving me something else to worry about while I still feel like shit is a great way to speed recovery. Whatever I said, I don't want to know, assuming it wasn't all gibberish anyway."

Ezhil just smirked in that infuriating way of his. "Whatever you wish, Your Highness."

"The very second I'm capable of standing up…"

"Oh, knock it off, you two," Vyra said with a laugh. "I can see this relationship is always going to be you two snarking and sniping at each other because Night forbid you flirt any other way, and me breaking it up." He laughed again. "You're lucky I find it charming."

Tashi was still too groggy to make any

sense of what they were saying. "I need to piss." He finished the cup of tea, ignoring the way it nearly burned his tongue, and shuffled out of bed, waving off Ezhil's attempts to help—and regretting everything when he put weight on his feet. "Fuck."

"I tried to tell you," Ezhil said with a huff. "Are you forgetting what put you in bed in the first place?"

"No," Tashi said, though all three of them could very much hear the *yes*. Huffing, he sat more comfortably on the edge of the bed. "Where's my jewelry?"

Ezhil grabbed the bag from where it lay the fireplace mantel and brought it to him. "We took it off for safekeeping; I hope we didn't do anything wrong."

"It would take a lot of skill and effort to do something wrong in putting jewelry back in the bag. I'm more concerned what I might have done to my gloves."

"There was a small tear in one, but nothing that can't be easily stitched." Ezhil sat down next to him. "I wasn't certain ordinary thread would work, though."

"Mage silk thread is always best, but ordinary thread will work just fine. I can do it, though; it's not your job—"

"Oh, shush," Vyra said. "You can't even walk, and you don't have to do everything by yourself anymore."

Tashi pinched his eyes shut and took a deep breath. "All right, I feel like there's a conversation happening here that I'm missing pieces of. First, though, I need to treat my feet and take a fucking piss."

Ezhil snickered, Vyra smiled, and they both withdrew as Tashi bent to his tasks.

Several minutes later, feeling more or less human again, he reclaimed his seat on the edge of the bed and started working on the marvelous smelling stew someone had made. "So why do you two keep talking like the three of us are…"

"Lovers?" Ezhil finished.

Tashi flinched, because yes, that was what he'd been thinking, but he distinctly recalled not being part of a certain kiss. "It's no business of mine what the two of you get up to."

"Oh, for love of Night." Ezhil strode up to the bed, pushed Tashi down on it and straddled him, then bent and took his mouth.

Well. Fuck.

If anyone had told him days ago that he'd be kissing the one bastard in Ossiri that he most wanted to pitch into the river, Tashi would have laughed his ass off as he walked away to get on with his day.

He absolutely would not have imagined himself sinking fingers into Ezhil's surprisingly soft hair and feeding at his mouth like it would fix his every problem. His lips were ridiculously soft too, far softer than they had any damn business being. Ezhil tasted sweet, like he'd put entirely too much honey in his tea.

When they finally drew apart, Tashi let out a breathy, "Well, fuck me."

"If you insist."

Tashi laughed even as he rolled his eyes. "Get off. Let me up. You're out of your mind." He looked at Vyra, who was watching them intently, eyes hotter than any fire. "You both are." Ezhil stood and helped Tashi to his feet, but before Tashi could say anything further, Vyra was stepping into his space and resting a hand along the side of his face. "Ezhil and I want to kill each other on a good day, and you've known me a handful of days and Ezhil less than that."

"I know when something or someone smells right, human," Vyra replied, the most feral thing he'd ever said, and took a kiss of his own. He was toothier than Tashi had expected, but exactly as quietly commanding as anticipated, allowing Tashi to do nothing but delightfully submit. He tasted like tea, as well, but not nearly as sweet as Ezhil.

Tashi was panting lightly when they finally drew apart. "It's always the quiet ones."

Vyra rubbed his lips with a thumb, then said, "Come on, let's eat. You need to rebuild the strength lost by the fever. To judge by that downpour, we'll have plenty of time for you to do so."

Tashi huffed but obeyed, though he was

more than happy at the slight delay of watching Ezhil twine around Vyra for a kiss of his own. "So what made you two kiss by the fire last night?"

Pulling apart, Vyra gave him a look. "Didn't know you'd seen that until you started rambling in the midst of your fever."

Tashi's face burned hot. "I never want to know what I said. I mean that."

"Understood, but it was all quite adorable," Ezhil said with an unrepentant grin. Though really, did he have any other kind? "It happened because I told Vyra that if he didn't hurry up and kiss you, I'd do it myself. Then the crafty bastard kissed *me*. I'm starting to think he's been planning this for a while."

"It's only you ridiculous humans who think everything has to be done in pairs. Now sit down and eat."

Ezhil laughed and obeyed, and with a smile of his own, Tashi followed suit. His feet were still sore, but infinitely better than they had been, and after a few more days of proper rest they'd be as good as new. What he'd do for shoes the rest of the journey was a problem he'd figure out later.

Vyra put a bowl teeming with stew in front of him, making Tashi's stomach rumble again. He took a bite and moaned. "Whoever made this, it's delicious."

"Me," Ezhil said, looking more pleased than Tashi had ever seen him.

As Tashi started on his second bowl of stew and third piece of bread, he asked, "So what exactly do you mean when you say we 'smell right'? I've heard that before, though rarely, but never known what it means exactly. Just the usual nonsense about ferals having one true mate and all that."

Vyra snorted and reached up absently to rub at one of his shorn horns. "Many feral families, where humans won't judge and bother us anyway, often have one husband and anywhere from two to five wives, though two to three is most common. So no, we don't have 'one true mate.' I'm not a fucking swan."

Tashi and Ezhil burst into laughter, poorly muffling it with their hands or arms.

"To answer your question," Vyra said dryly over their racket, "it's hard to describe. It's the way you can stay in nice hotels, beautiful campsites, the finest nomad wagon… even a fancy palace, and enjoy every single moment… but you still get this simple feeling of happy and right when you step into your own home again. There are typical smells, strange smells, bad, good… right. I don't know how else to say it."

Tashi swallowed, levity fading. "I think you said it perfectly. I didn't realize…"

Vyra shrugged. "It wasn't for you to know, not when we could have simply gone our separate ways and never seen each other again. Trust me when I say I wasn't expecting such a scent to come first from a body catcher, and then from a body snatcher that you have some strange love-hate relationship with. It's been a bizarre series of days, and I sense everything will get even stranger before this particular adventure is over."

Ezhil pushed from the table and rose. "Personally, I'm hoping that now we're out of sight, we're out of mind."

"They think I'm trying to murder my mother via a slow-acting curse," Tashi said with a snort. "This is far from over."

"Well, it's on hold for the moment, at least. Now shall we move on to more pleasant matters?"

Vyra rolled his eyes. "I'm sure Tashi would like a proper bath, and *you* can go get more firewood while I deal with the dishes."

Ezhil pouted but obeyed, and Tashi went off to the door Vyra pointed to and found, to his pleasant surprise, an entire washroom. "I really like this cabin. It's much more than I was expecting."

"I've always been a bit fond of it," Vyra replied as he finished up the dishes and washed and dried his hands. He tossed the towel aside and added, "Come here."

Tashi had never been so delighted to follow an order in his life and twined his arms around Vyra's neck as he was pulled close, happily submitting to the slow, leisurely kiss he was given. After all the times he'd spent admiring Vyra's strength, he was desperately eager to see what it was like in bed. He also couldn't wait to learn all new ways of shutting Ezhil up and driving him crazy.

Drawing back, Vyra said, "Shall we give Ezhil something delightful to walk in on?"

Tashi kissed Vyra again, then drew back enough to say, "I think that sounds like a wonderful idea."

Chapter Fourteen

"You're just agreeing because you know it'll drive him mad," Vyra replied dryly, even as he dragged Tashi to the bed. "Clothes off, Your Highness. I'd like to be able to enjoy the view this time, now I'm not worried that you're going to die on us."

"Stop calling me that," Tashi said with a sigh, but drew his shirt over his head and cast it aside.

Vyra stepped into his space again and ran a hand over his chest, making Tashi's skin prickle. "You could do with more meat on your bones, but you really are lovely."

"We could all do with more meat," Tashi said. "That's life in the Rotter." The words turned breathless at the end as Vyra moved in closer, hands moving to span across his back, one tracing the line of his spine, as Vyra's lips traced whisper soft along his jaw. He settled his own hands on Vyra's broad shoulders, tipping his head to one side to give those soft lips better access to his throat, shivering at the teasing drag of sharp teeth. One hand dropped to cup his ass, and Tashi did some exploring of his own, enjoying the ripple of muscle as he smoothed his hands down Vyra's strong arms, imagining all the delightful things such strength could do.

Vyra kissed him again, slowly, leisurely, as if Tashi was his and he had all the time in the world to enjoy his prize. "You taste sweet, my prince, I don't know why that surprises me."

Of all the reactions in the world, Tashi blushed. "Stop calling me things like that! I'm not royalty anymore!"

"Maybe we just enjoy it's our little secret," Vyra said with a smirk, and cut off his reply with another kiss, twining a hand into Tashi's hair and holding him right where he wanted, leaving Tashi helpless to do anything but submit.

"Bossy," Tashi whispered when he was finally able to speak again.

Vyra just laughed and nudged him. "On the bed, facing the door."

"That sounds promising." Tashi did as told, losing the rest of his clothes along the way, leaving them scattered across the floor where he'd probably be annoyed by the dust and dirt later. "I don't suppose this place has better clothes I can steal?"

"In the loft—we'll check later." Vyra settled behind him, spreading Tashi's legs a bit wider before settling between them. He ran his hands, large and warm, along Tashi's back, down to his thighs, hands fitting to them perfectly, like Tashi had been carved for his touch, leaving him groaning, cock growing hard and heavy.

Sharp teeth sank into the meat of his left ass check, making him jerk, swear. "Bossy *and* toothy."

"You're not complaining, and I'm feral, remember? The bitey rumors are mostly true."

"You seemed so sweet when we met. Guess I should have known better of a man who traveled so far and worked so hard to break his sister out of an asylum." Tashi laughed. "Wonder what the sister's like."

Vyra laughed. "How is any woman who survives all the brutal nonsense men inflict on them? It doesn't matter, though, because you're mine, not hers."

"Believe me, that was never—" Tashi swore as he got a bite to the other cheek "—in doubt." He moaned, head dropping, as teeth were replaced with rough tongue, dragging along his skin like some strange combination of silk and sandpaper. "Fuck, don't do that. Do it more."

More laughter washed over his skin,

followed by another lick from that evil tongue, reducing Tashi to moans and panting pleas. Vyra dragged his tongue up and then down Tashi's spine, back over the stinging bites, one hand braced on the bed, the other teasing along his skin.

"I know you had a terrible time when you first came to the Rotter," Vyra said, "but do you have any good memories of... intimate moments?"

Tashi frowned, some of the delighted haze fading. "I don't think so, not really. Good sex wasn't exactly rare in my world, I guess, but... it was a means to an end, or a way to alleviate boredom. Then abruptly it became a way to not die, then to pay bills. I'm not sure I ever fucked anyone just because I wanted to, because I sincerely cared about the other person... or people... involved."

"I'm sorry." Vyra kissed the base of his spine, bringing back the shivers of too much, not enough. Before he could speak again, the words were cut off by the opening of the door, the appearance of Ezhil with an armload of wood.

Wood that went tumbling everywhere. "You bloody jerks!" He kicked the door shut and all but threw his cloak across the room before striding up to the foot of the bed. "You started without me. Fuck, you're pretty on your hands and knees, Your Highness."

Tashi tried to give a suitable retort to that, but the hands on his thighs reduced him to a helpless moan.

Ezhil smirked. "No, I will not stop calling you that." He pulled off his shirt and tossed it to join the rest of the clothes on the floor, then followed suit with his boots, pants, and underclothes, ending with pulling the tie from his hair, sending the dark red tresses tumbling all about.

Whimpering, Tashi managed, "How did I wind up with two redheads? That doesn't seem fair."

"Lucky or unlucky, you decide," Ezhil said, voice rougher than Tashi had ever heard it, sending fresh shivers of *want* and *need* down his spine. "Fuck, you're pretty, Tashi. I know people who would commit murder in front of the guards just for a chance to *touch* you."

Tashi managed a ragged laugh that turned into another long, needy moan as Vyra pushed a slick finger inside him. "Luck—fuck—lucky for you, you get it for free. Are you going to keep standing there running your stupid mouth or do something?"

That got him a noise impressively close to a growl for a human, and then Ezhil was stroking his own cock, his other hand curling into Tashi's disheveled hair. "Do you know how many times I've pretended not to want to know how you look with your stupidly pretty mouth wrapped around my cock?"

Grinning as best he could while Vyra's

fingers continued to tease and stretch him, Tashi said, "Let's find out, shall we?"

Ezhil's eyes were full of fire as he tightened his grip in Tashi's hair and slowly fed his cock into Tashi's mouth, breath coming out in sharp, ragged groans as Tashi sucked him in deep, tongue stroking all he could reach. "Fuck, you're pretty."

Tashi couldn't deny he liked the praise. The *sincerity* of the praise, when he was used to only the forced compliments of people wanting to please a bratty prince, or customers hoping he would lower the price if they were nice enough.

One finger became two, Vyra stretching him wide, and Tashi pulled off Ezhil's cock to shudder and gasp, breathing heavily against his skin, head pressed against his hip.

"Back to work, pretty prince," Ezhil said, though he sounded only fond and faintly amused. "You're not here because of your wit."

"Shut up, you stupid bastard," Tashi said, and went back to sucking his cock as Vyra pushed him to taking three fingers, moaning at the stretch in his ass and his mouth, the hands that stroked soothingly along his spine in sharp counterpoint to the tight hold on his hair and the fingers buried in his ass. So much sensation. Too much. Not enough. He wanted them to fuck him. Use him. Leave him sore and wrung out. *Wanted*, when he couldn't remember the last time he'd felt like someone even liked him.

He pulled off Ezhil's cock a second time,

panting against his skin, as Vyra finally pushed inside of him, hard and thick, stretching him wide despite the thorough preparations. Tashi kissed Ezhil's skin, soft and salty, so very warm, panting hard as Vrya finished filling him.

"Never seen anything more beautiful in my life," Vyra said hoarsely.

"Agreed," Ezhil said, voice just as rough. "Fuck, Tashi. You were made for pleasure. It's a crime you don't run the entire pleasure district."

Tashi didn't know how to respond to that, so he simply went back to sucking Ezhil's cock as Vyra started to move inside him, pulling out just enough to thrust back in, sending him rocking forward, taking Ezhil's cock even deeper, setting all three of them to moaning, begging for more while also praising each other, filling the cabin with the sounds of unchecked pleasure, the rest of the world so far away it may as well not exist.

He could not remember the last time he'd enjoyed sex so much, not after it had become a means of survival, a way to not die starved and alone on the streets. Sex had always been a means to an end, and pleasure an unexpected bonus.

Ezhil's hands gripped his hair, wrapped around his head, holding him firmly in place as he fucked Tashi's mouth with shameless abandon, while Vyra plowed his ass with increasing fervor, noisy pants growing louder and louder, the hands on his hips gripping with almost bruising tightness.

The flexing of Ezhil's fingers, his long moan, signaled the climax that came a moment later, as Ezhil pushed deep into his throat and spilled. Tashi took all of it, pulled off his cock slowly, licking and suckling as he went, until he could drop his head between his shoulders and focus on the pounding Vyra was still giving him, gripping the footboard to keep himself from going too far forward and toppling right off the edge.

Vyra grunted and sank into him, folding his body to Tashi's, holding him tightly as he came. Tashi moaned, aching and desperate, possibly whimpering as Vyra pulled out of him.

In the next breath he was on his back, with Ezhil kissing him senseless, teasing at his skin, flicking his nipples, as Vyra got a hand around his cock and stroked him hard and quick, until Tashi came with a shout, trembling in their arms as the world whited out around him.

When he could more or less function again, he was sprawled out in the middle of the bed, Ezhil curled up close behind him, Vyra stretched out not quite touching on the other side. "This… is an impressively big bed."

"Think somebody with a large family who passed through built it with that in mind. Certainly works out for the rest of us."

Tashi closed his eyes, mouth curved in a smile. "I really do like this place. It's charming, and so well located. Plenty of land, room to build a boarding house, you could…" He broke off with a yawn, then shook himself. "Why am I so tired again? I just woke up."

"You were just thoroughly fucked too, you stupid body catcher," Ezhil said, and pressed a soft kiss to the side of throat. "Go to sleep."

"If you insist," Tashi said around another yawn, and was asleep just moments later.

When he woke sometime later in need of a piss, the large room was dark and quiet, the only noise and light coming from the fire across the room. All this quiet was going to take getting used to after years of living in a city that never entirely slept.

Carefully dislodging Ezhil's arm, he squirmed and nudged his way out of the pile of warm limbs he was trapped under and went to relieve himself.

"There you are," Ezhil grumbled as he returned to the bed. "Thought you might have wandered off to overthink and sulk."

"Just needed to piss," Tashi replied, and gave in to the need to kiss him, even as he still grappled with the fact that he wanted, *needed*, to kiss Ezhil. "A few days ago I would have gladly thrown you into the Oss."

Ezhil snickered against his mouth. "Don't worry, the urge will return. It's not like you've stopped being an obnoxious brat who thinks he's the best body catcher in the city."

"I am—was—the best body catcher in the city."

"Shut up," Ezhil said, kisses turning sharper, hungrier. "Why didn't I ever think to do this sooner? I want to fuck you, let me fuck you—"

Tashi meant to sound exasperated, but the words came out amused instead. "No, you two have used me enough, and you're going to wake up—"

"Oh, I'm already awake, and now you're going to have to make being awake worth it," Vyra said in a deep, sleep-soaked voice that finished the job of waking up Tashi's cock. He grabbed hold of Tashi and turned him, pulled him close, hitching one of Tashi's legs up over his own massive thigh, spreading him nicely open.

"I'm pretty certain I said—" Tashi broke off with a whimpering moan as Ezhil pushed easily inside him, breaths hot and heavy on his neck. "Fuck."

"Yes, that's what we're doing, good job, Your Highness."

"I hate you so much," Tashi said between moans, clinging to Vyra, rutting against him as Ezhil fucked him in slow, easy strokes, as though he had all the time in the world and was going to use every last second.

A hand wrapped around his cock, and Vyra's mouth found his, sucking and biting at his lips in time with Ezhil's thrusts. Tashi fumbled between their bodies until he found Vyra's cock, matching the rhythm the other two had set to stroke Vyra in turn, until the three of them came together in a big messy, sweaty pile, groans filling the room.

"Please tell me we don't have to be up early to resume traveling," Tashi panted out as they slowly, stiffly untangled. "I think I need another bath."

Vyra laughed and rolled out of bed. "I'll draw the water and get it heating."

"Guess I may as well see about tea and a bite to eat," Ezhil said, climbing out of his side of the bed.

"I'm staying right here," Tashi replied. "The next time we do this, someone else's ass gets a turn."

That just got him a round of entirely too smug laughter that he refused to acknowledge.

"Here," Vyra said once the water was ready, "I'll help Your Highness—"

"Oh, Night, quit it, seriously." Tashi rolled his eyes as he shuffled slowly to the washroom, entire body sore but not in a bad way for once, though his feet still ached, despite his work healing them. He settled into the hot water with a groan. "Stop calling me Your Highness."

"No," Ezhil retorted. "Give up."

Tashi just sighed and took the soap Vyra offered. "So when—"

He stopped at the sound of voices. Several of them, coming from the back of the cabin. "Who the fuck is that?"

"Travelers or bandits, but who can say which?" Vyra replied, voice pitched low. "Shall I go investigate?"

Ezhil shot him a look. "Yes, go outside in the dead of night to see if unexpected visitors are safe or dangerous. Good plan."

"Well, it's better than letting them come inside," Vyra retorted. "I can handle myself just fine."

"Shut up both of you," Tashi said, mind racing as he tried to think and the voices grew louder, closer. So much for having a bath, a snack, and going back to sleep.

Chapter Fifteen

"Check it out, Vyra," Tashi said. "If it's fellow travelers, you can help them outside while we clean up in here. If it's a small problem, deal with it. If it's a bigger problem, come back inside. By then I'll have my jewelry." Also hopefully some clothes, as he really did not want to get into a fight bare ass naked.

Ezhil did not look remotely happy with his edict, but said nothing as Vyra went to investigate, only retrieved his own clothes while Tashi went for his jewelry first.

Tashi had just managed to pull on his pants when the door slammed open and Vyra came stumbling in, blood pouring from a wound on his head. "Bandits," he said, stumbling, nearly hitting the floor before Ezhil caught him. "The bastards from earlier. They must have managed to trail us or just made a good guess about where we'd stop."

"Persistent assholes," Tashi muttered. "Leave this to me. Give me your shirt."

Ezhil immediately pulled his shirt off and handed it over before returning his full attention to Vyra.

No shoes, but his dick wasn't hanging out, so Tashi would take it. The jewelry was all that really mattered.

Opening the door, he stepped outside just as the bandits were converging and threw out a cantrip for fire before they even registered he wasn't Vyra again.

He caught three of them, sending them into panicked flailing as they tried to put themselves out. Three down, five to go.

The man in charge, the one who'd demanded Tashi's jewelry before, stepped over what remained of the flames. "I was hoping to see you again."

Tashi called up wind but didn't release the cantrip. "You don't know who you're messing with. Leave or you'll end this night dead."

Laughing meanly, the man replied, "I've dealt with warlocks before, boy."

"That's not what I'm talking about." Tashi threw the cantrip, sending a blast of wind at the remaining group, sticks and leaves and other detritus flying, along with water from the storm that had temporarily abated. Before they could push past it, he surged down the steps and punched the leader in the face, then stole his sword as he reeled back.

After that, the rest was easy.

"Who the fuck are you?" the leader demanded as his life bled away.

"A body catcher from the Rotter." Tashi tossed the sword and wiped blood from his face as the rain started to fall again. "Enjoy feeding the wildlife." He waited until the man was dead, confirmed he was dead, then checked on all the others.

By the time he returned to the cabin, he was soaked though, but at least the blood had washed away. He stripped off his clothes, now beyond all hope of redemption.

"Drive them off?" Ezhil asked.

"Killed them," Tashi said flatly. "I was nice the first time. They had their chance. Half-penny robbers like that shouldn't mess with the Rotter."

Vyra gave him a look from where he was sipping tea by the fire. "Pretty sure being a warlock helped."

"Magic emphasizes defense and protection above all else, even if our armies would have you think otherwise. I didn't learn to kill being royalty, right up until I did it. That death is cheap and easy… that I learned in the Rotter."

"Yeah," Ezhil said with a sigh. "That's the Rotter."

"Can't argue that," Vyra added quietly. "Get washed up: there's clean water, though not heated."

Tashi scoffed even as Vyra rolled his eyes at his own words, like Tashi hadn't heated the water for them before. Doing so now, he then slid into the water with a groan. "How's your head?"

"Fine. Just a melodramatic scratch at the end of the day." Vyra finished his tea and took the cup to the washing bin, then crossed to the tub. "How are you?"

"They never laid a finger on me. Got cocky. Thought they'd gotten you, and since I'd run before, that I wouldn't be a challenge. I'll need to deal with the bodies, but it's gonna have to wait until the rain stops."

Ezhil gagged. "The bodies can stay where they are. I'm not moving bodies bloated by water, no thank you. Did that twice, and that was two times too many."

"You don't have magic," Tashi said with a laugh. "Levitation cantrips are damned useful for moving bodies in poor condition."

"Show off," Ezhil retorted.

Smirking, Tashi heaved out of the water, letting most of it drain away before climbing out of the tub and accepting the towel Vyra handed him. "Thanks." He oofed slightly as he was reeled in, but fell gladly into the kiss Vyra gave him, enjoying the taste of tea and honey and Ezhil that lingered in his mouth. When they drew apart, he brushed his fingers over Vyra's wound. "Shall I heal it?"

"No, it's fine. Not everything needs magic, Your Highness."

Tashi sighed. "I hear that more now than I did when I was royalty."

Ezhil snickered as he brought Tashi what looked to be a battered old dressing robe. "Here, found this up in the loft. Clothes, too. A little big, but we can fix them up before we leave, since you still need some proper rest before pushing those feet any harder. Yes, I know you healed them, but rest anyway. It's not like we can go anywhere until the weather clears up and some of the water dries, unless you want to slog through mud and muck."

"Not really, no," Tashi said, shrugging into the robe. "Though the longer we hold still, the likelier my sister will find us."

Vyra shrugged. "I still think that if we're out of sight, we're out of mind. If not, there's not really anything we can do about it. If she can find us here, she can find us in the feral encampment. We can only do what we can do."

"Stop being reasonable." Tashi belted the robe closed, shooting Ezhil a warning look. "You're not touching my ass again already. I'm hungry and tired and want to look at these clothes you found."

"Shoes too," Ezhil said, before catching hold of him and dragging him into a sharp, hungry kiss. "Glad you're in one piece."

"Glad we're *all* fine," Tashi replied against his lips before taking another kiss, ignoring the way his stupid cock tried to stir. Tearing away, he turned his attention back to the clothes.

Mercifully, they were in good condition, only a little too big, and infinitely more practical than the clothes he'd borrowed before leaving Ossiri. "I can't believe there's so much stuff just lying around."

At the table where he was making them all more tea, Vyra replied, "People really do treat this as an unofficial waypoint. I can only imagine how it would flourish if someone had the money and inclination to make it official."

"Certainly sounds better than catching bodies," Tashi said. "Is there a sewing—" He frowned as Ezhil snatched the clothes away from him. "Give those back."

"Drink your tea, eat your food, and get back in that bed," Ezhil said. "You look two steps from falling over. You're still recovering from whatever made you sick, remember, on top of being taken thorough advantage of and killing like, what, eight men?"

"Thereabouts," Tashi replied, the word overtaken by a yawn. "Fine, fine." Under dual watchful gazes, he drank his tea, ate the bread, cheese, and dried fruit put in front of him, and shuffled back to bed.

Where, to be fair, he fell asleep almost immediately.

~~*

He woke hours later to sunlight and the delightful sound of skin slapping against skin, punctuated by breathy moans and stuttering pleas for more. Opening his eyes, muffling a yawn in his arm, he stared across the room at the delightful sight of Ezhil bent over the table while Vyra fucked him hard enough the table shifted slightly a couple of times.

Well, that was certainly a morning greeting he could get used to. Throwing back the blankets, Tashi climbed out of bed and went around to where he could watch Ezhil's face as Vyra plowed him, the way he scrabbled at the table for purchase he could never entirely find. "That's a pretty sight."

Ezhil's eyes snapped open, and he grinned. "Here to serve, Your Highness."

"You wouldn't serve if someone paid you," Tashi retorted, as he got his own cock out and stroked it idly while he watched them. The way their faces scrunched with effort, the sweat dripping down their flushed skin. Vyra's hands tight on Ezhil's hips as he fucked him deep and hard. Tashi groaned as he stroked his own cock harder, shuddering as Ezhil came, as Vyra kept fucking him a few more moments before coming himself.

Sinking to his knees, almost more falling,

Ezhil said, "Come here."

Tashi obeyed happily, standing in front of Ezhil, sinking one hand into his hair as he pushed his cock between those pretty lips. Ezhil licked and sucked with no small skill, even better than the previous night, and it wasn't long at all before Tashi was coming with a long groan, spilling down his throat, hand tight in his soft, fiery-red hair.

He sank to the floor to sit beside Ezhil, slowly catching his breath. "Your mouth."

"It keeps me alive as often as it gets me in trouble, that's for sure," Ezhil said with a grin. "You seem to be feeling better."

"By leagues. Did I miss breakfast?"

"There's some left for you." Vyra helped them to their feet, kissing each of them and swatting their asses. "Come on, work to do. I've got your clothes adjusted, I think, Your Highness. I'll leave you and your fancy tricks to deal with those bodies."

"I am the one that killed them, so that seems fair." Tashi went to the foot of the bed, where Vyra had pointed, and pulled on the clothes waiting for him. They smelled faintly of dust, but were warm and soft as he pulled them on and laced everything in place. Sitting down, he picked up the boots that had sat alongside the bench. "Are these mine, too?"

Vyra nodded. "Yeah. Lots of shoes up there. I think people just leave whatever they don't need or can't carry. They could do with resoling, but they'll more than suffice until we reach the encampment."

"I appreciate it," Tashi said as he pulled on socks and boots. Properly dressed at last, he tugged Vyra in and kissed him deeply, still reeling faintly that he was allowed to do this. Kiss Vyra. Kiss Ezhil. Have them both however he liked. How had he gone from nothing and no one to these two?

It seemed fragile, like it might be snatched away at any moment.

Pulling away, he nuzzled Vyra's cheek and then withdrew completely. "Guess I'd better get to work."

Outside, the bodies were already beginning to smell, and that smell was not pleasant. For better or worse, it was also familiar, though. He didn't have many skills, but he had magic, and he could dispose of bodies. What a combination.

Breathing as shallowly as he could get away with, Tashi went to each body, stripped it of anything useful, and cast the cantrip for levitation. Once he had them all hovering in the air, he nudged them to the edge of the canyon. One by one he pushed them to hover over the canyon, like the world's most disgusting clouds. With a snap of his fingers, he broke the cantrips and watched as the bodies plummeted out of sight.

How much easier his job back in the Rotter would have been with a handy canyon nearby. Ah, well. He had the feeling he was retired now, so it little mattered.

Gathering up his contraband, he carried it all into the house and deposited it on the table.

"Oh, what have we here?" Ezhil asked, abandoning whatever he was cooking on the stove to join Tashi in rifling through bags, pouches, weapons, and more. "Nice haul."

"Where's Vyra?" Tashi asked as he divided the knives into four piles. One pile for each of them, and the remainder to leave at the cabin. He did the same with the swords. "Can you even use a sword?"

"No, not even a little. Vyra should be up in the loft. He wanted to see what else was there, look for stuff he could use to make a couple of repairs around here before we leave."

Tashi nodded and set two swords aside. He wasn't really all that good with a sword, but he had the same basic training any noble went through, and recent events had proven they were useful to have. Magic couldn't solve every problem, alas.

Weapons out of the way, he moved on to the pouches, while Ezhil dealt with the bags.

Medicine powders, useful. Coins, even more useful. Firestarter, tinder, tin of spices, sharpening stone, candy, two pouches of tobacco, rolling paper, and a pipe. "Good haul."

"You're telling me. Bet they have horses somewhere too." Ezhil dropped the last of the empty bags on a chair and went through the contents, which proved to be a map, more coins, more tobacco and requisite supplies for it, cooking tools, two cheap books, a set of panpipes, some foodstuffs, spare clothes that smelled absolutely rank, and various bits of jewelry that had probably been stolen from other travelers.

"What's all this, then?" Vyra asked as he came down from the loft hauling wood and a battered tool bag.

"Took it off the robbers. Kept a sword for you. Figure that pile can all remain here. Clothes, too, after we wash them and go through them all."

Vyra nodded. "Let me fix the south wall and the wood bin, and I can help."

Tashi waved him off. "I can handle laundry. You get repairs; Ezhil is feeding us. Tomorrow we can head out."

"Solid plan." Ezhil kissed him, then Vyra, before returning to his bubbling stewpot.

Vyra took a kiss from Tashi, then headed off with a smile.

With a smile of his own lingering, Tashi gathered up all the laundry and hauled it outside, where he found exactly what he needed behind the cabin. Filling the large tub propped against the back wall, he filled it and heated the water to nearly boiling. A cabinet beneath the window revealed soap that he added, and once the water was ready, he tossed in the clothes and got to scrubbing.

He'd just finished with the scrubbing when he heard the pounding of hooves on hard-packed earth. Abandoning the laundry, Tashi went back around the house to the front just as the rider reached it. His chest tightened as he noted the royal livery the man wore, the marks on his jacket that said he'd been serving for at least twenty years, the gray hair that hinted it was probably far longer than that.

Pulling to a halt, the man dismounted and headed for the house—and stopped short as he finally noticed Tashi. His eyes widened with recognition, but before he could speak, Tashi surged forward, grabbed the man by the scruff of his shirt, and slammed him into the wall. Pulling a knife, he held it to the man's throat."

"Please, no! I'm not here to cause trouble! I swear! I promise! Don't kill me, please!"

"You work for my sister," Tashi hissed, because this close, he could see the perched lark that was his sister's personal crest.

The door opened, and Tashi could hear the other two rushing toward them, but he didn't take his eyes off the man, pressing the knife even more firmly to his throat.

"Who is that?" Vyra asked.

"Personal scout for my sister," Tashi bit out.

Ezhil made a derisive noise. "Then best get rid of him, I'd think."

"He may know something useful," Vyra replied.

"Please don't kill me," the man replied. "I'm just—"

"Shut up," Tashi said, weighing his options.

Chapter Sixteen

Killing the bastard would slow down whatever trouble his sister was causing now, but Tashi had never enjoyed killing and didn't want to do it if he didn't have to. "One suspicious movement and you're done," he said as he let the man go. "What mission are you on?"

"Just delivering a message to various parties," the man said, flexing and relaxing his fingers at his side, eyes darting around everywhere before he finally met Tashi's gaze. "I did not expect to see Your Highness, not after all this time. They always said you were dead, until… all this. Um, but, my news is this: Her Majesty the Queen is dead, felled by a curse. Many still believe you to be the culprit behind the deed, but I think nearly as many wonder if that's true. I was to deliver the news to several parties in the south."

Tashi could guess which ones, and they were irrelevant to him. "Any other news?"

"Your sister is to be crowned Queen in five days. There is still a bounty on your head. The city is… not doing well."

"Where is my sister right now?"

"I left yesterday, was slowed by the storm, but when I left, she was in the palace and had given no indications she'd be traveling."

"Anything else?"

"No, Your Highness. That was the sum of my message, and the sum of my knowledge."

"I'm not a prince anymore," Tashi finally said. "It's just Tashi now. Thank you. Sorry for assaulting you. These past days have been… difficult. Get food, some rest, and be on your way."

Leaving the scout and his lovers, Tashi returned to the back of the cabin, but instead of resuming his work, he sat down on an old stump and simply stared at the fields beyond.

His mother was dead.

He'd agreed to save her life, and ruined his own hard-won life in the process, and had failed.

His mother was dead. His sister still wanted him dead for it.

So much lost. So much violence. So much pain. All to fail.

His sister would soon be queen. Once upon a time, he would have resented he was not there to be her Warlock Prime. All he felt now was a deep sense of relief. He didn't enjoy struggling for every coin, living a life and job that would someday get him arrested or killed, but he would be damned if he went back to the slow-poison life of a royal prince.

Footsteps drew his attention, and he turned to see Ezhil approaching. "Would have thought Vyra would appoint you watchdog."

"Me too, but he said go, so I went," Ezhil said. "Are you wishing you were home right now?"

"Actually relieved I'm not. I can only imagine how much worse of a person I would be if I'd remained in that world all this time. All I want right now is for my sister to leave us alone." He looked up as Ezhil stood in front of him, reaching out to trail his fingers along one thigh before curling them around it. "Be nice to settle somewhere, instead of being on the run like this. I get the feeling from how little Vyra has said about it, that we'll be tolerated amongst the Ferals but not exactly welcomed with open arms or encouraged to stay."

"Don't think we'd be too welcome back in the city."

"I wouldn't be, but I think you two would be fine in time."

"Well, we're three now, somehow, even if

I'm still not sure how I wound up with the world's most aggravating body catcher."

"You have no grounds for calling someone else aggravating," Tashi replied with a faint smile. He tugged until Ezhil knelt in front of him, where Tashi could kiss him. He still couldn't quite believe that *he* was kissing *Ezhil*, but he was more than happy to keep doing it.

When they eventually drew apart, Ezhil said, "I am sorry about your mother. Nobody deserves to die so horribly."

"If anyone did, it was her," Tashi said. "Let's not forget that she threw me out because I killed a rapist. Her solution to that problem was to let her son die on the street, when she could have solved the problem any other way." He sighed. "Wish I knew what really drove her to do it. Ever since you asked the obvious, it's troubled me."

Ezhil kissed him again, soft, like the flutter of a butterfly's wings. "I wouldn't worry about it. If I had to guess, I'd say she didn't like you possibly being more popular than your sister. Parents like that really hate when their golden child isn't as loved as their least favorite. You see it all the time. I can only imagine how much nastier such things get at that level. Night, I've seen it happen when I'm hired to get rid of the bodies of children, usually boys that died of 'unknown illness' or 'mysteriously in their sleep' because the parents wanted a daughter, not another son."

"True enough." Tashi sighed. "I suppose we should—" He stopped as the feel of magic rose sharply, standing up suddenly enough he sent Ezhil toppling, and turned around just in time to see the column of blinding green light that shot up into the sky. "Damn it!"

He bolted for the cabin, throwing the door open and tumbling inside. He swept the room, saw Vyra unconscious, and then located the backstabbing scout. "You!"

"I didn't have a choice—" the scout said, even as Tashi slammed him into the wall much like he had before, and this time the knife he pressed to the bastard's throat drew blood. "She'll kill my family if I don't—"

Tashi snarled, dropped his knife, and cast a cantrip that knocked the man out cold. Leaving him crumpled on the floor, he went to look over Vyra.

"What in the world is going on?" Ezhil asked, looking from the unconscious scout to the column of light by the fireplace that cut through the roof as though it wasn't there, continuing on up into the sky until it faded from sight.

"Beacon," Tashi said tersely as he looked Vyra over. Thankfully, he only looked as though he'd been put to sleep, likely struck with a spell when he'd turned away for one second. "That fucking scout cast a beacon. My sister will be here any minute, and there is fuck all I can do about it."

Ezhil sighed. "Told you to kill the bastard. Is Vyra all right?"

"Just out cold, I'll wake him up. Make us all some tea, would you?"

A few minutes later, they were all gathered around the table. "You can't just put the beacon out or something?"

"No, unfortunately not." Tashi held his mug in both hands, enjoying the warmth, the sweetness of the fragrant tea. "It's powerful magic, and can't be canceled until united with the other half. This part is called the 'mark'; the other half is the 'call'. When the call is placed in the mark, the beacon goes out." He glanced to where Vyra had rather vindictively tied the scout to one of the posts around the room. "Guess that's what I get for being nice. You two could still run, though. My sister won't have any interest in you so long as she has me."

"You can't be sure of that," Vyra replied, reaching across the table to take one of his hands, "and we're a team now, the three of us. We're not going anywhere."

Tashi nodded but couldn't bring himself to speak as he felt the tingling rush of rising magic. The beacon glowed brighter, turned blue. The light spread out, overtaking the room, forcing all of them to cover their eyes.

When it finally cleared, five people filled the room: Janashta, his sister; Rumér, who looked miserable to those who could read him; a stuffy-looking official Tashi didn't recognize; and two guards armed to the teeth.

"Would you like some tea, sister?" Tashi asked. "Don't expect us to pour it for you, though."

Janashta and her coterie looked glaringly out of place in the humble cabin, especially her, in velvet and silk and jewels that could buy the city three times over. Looking at all the extravagance made his stomach churn.

One of the guards went to stand by the door, blocking their exit, and the other stood just behind and beside Janashta as she sat at the head of the table. Rumér stood on her other side, casting Tashi a brief look of apology, probably because he was the only one who could have set up something as complicated as a beacon. Probably several, all sent in various directions, in the hopes one would work.

"I could kill you right here, right now, and nobody would give a single damn about you or your little friends here," Janashta said.

"Probably, but what I don't understand is why you're going to all this trouble. I haven't bothered any of you in all the years I've been living in the Rotter. Why do you care now? We both know I'm not the one who cursed Mother. I didn't have that kind of power until just yesterday, when I commandeered some jewelry."

"Yes, that will be addressed, at a later time," Janashta said icily. "The only thing that matters is that you're a threat to me, Tenzin, and I want you out of the way."

"If you'd just left me alone, I'd still be out of your way. I only got tangled up in all this because Rumér asked me to help find who was responsible for the curse. Like a fool, I agreed to help. All for nothing. Mother's dead and I don't have a fucking home anymore, or a job, or anything else. Why couldn't you just leave me alone? I'm not a threat. I never was, even when I was still your brother. My lone aspiration was to be your Warlock Prime. So why I am suddenly a threat to you after all these years?"

"Because you're the true heir," Ezhil said out of nowhere.

Janashta flinched visibly, something that Tashi had *never* seen from her.

"What are you talking about?" He stared at Ezhil, but his mind was entirely on that flinch. "We're a year and a half apart, give or take a month."

Ezhil looked between them again, and said, "Yeah, but are you certain you're the younger? Because looking at you both, if I'd been asked blind, I would have said *you* were older."

Tashi scoffed. "I've been living in the Rotter all these years. Ain't none of us look as young as we might if we were coddled brats in the palace."

"No, he's right," Vyra said, in that soft but forceful way of his. "Sitting here like this... I don't know how the secret was kept, but I would wager my life—which I guess I am, really—that you are older, and therefore the rightful king."

"That's crazy," Tashi said, even as his hands began to tremble. "It's a year and a half of difference, and I've been living rough for years. Of course I look older. Who could even tell with a difference that slight, anyway?" The churning in his stomach, though, growing worse by the second, belied his words.

It was the only thing that would explain why his mother had thrown him out over something she could have easily swept under the rug if she'd wanted. Ezhil was right, he'd always been right: nobility and royalty killed people all the time and got away with it. One murder by a royal prince of a noble wasn't enough to get him thrown out. Sent overseas for several years, maybe, but that was all.

But if he'd been born first, and proven to be a man once he was old enough to decide and declare that... If his sister had been born a little more than a year later... the queendom had always been ruled by women. Nobody wanted a king on the throne, according to everyone with power. Women were meant to rule, not men.

His mother had hidden it, switched them as soon as Janashta was old enough for the ruse to work. Now that he looked back, they hadn't even really interacted with each other until he was five or so, his sister six going on seven. When they were little, he'd always thought it funny that he was a little big for his age, and Janashta a little small for her age.

Fuck, he was stupid. Right in front of his face this whole *fucking* time, and it was Ezhil who'd noticed it with zero effort.

"So what, your plan is to kill me, hide the evidence, continue acting like you've always been the true firstborn and heir?" Tashi laughed bitterly. "All you had to do was *leave me alone*."

"I couldn't, not after Mother was cursed, and we couldn't find the fucking culprit, and—" She broke off, huffed. "A whole lot of other things that need not concern you. Blaming you was the best and easiest way to deal with the matter until we could find the real culprits."

"You could have *asked*, instead of going straight to murder, you jackass," Tashi snarled. "I should fucking kill *you* for all this madness and take my fucking throne!"

Both of the guards tensed, the one close to his sister even going for his sword, but Janashta motioned them to stand down. "But..."

"But I never fucking wanted it—how many times do I have to say that? All I ever wanted after getting thrown out like garbage was to never see any of you ever again. That hasn't changed, except I want to see you even *less* somehow." He huffed, opened his mouth to shout some more, but in the end closed it and subsided.

The silence lingered, until Rumér broke it by saying, "I have told this to Her Majesty, and the late Queen, many times. She promised she would discuss the matter with you, reasonably and fairly," he added, voice taking on an edge, "which is the only reason I agreed to make the beacons. I had little hope they'd work, but clearly the gamble paid off. I am sorry for all this, Tashi. I never should have gotten you involved."

Tashi sighed. "I wish I'd been able to solve the problem. I honestly don't give a damn if mother is dead, but I would have stopped the curse if I'd found it. I never thought I'd fail so abysmally."

"You didn't fail," Rumér said. "It was simply too late. You were right about those Circles of Frenzy being tied to the whole mess. I think they would have triggered with her death, but I was able to find and negate them all with relative ease—only because I knew what to look for, thanks to you. Without you, everything would have been so much worse, and countless people would be dead or injured right now."

"Also, it's not your fault you were turned into the scapegoat and couldn't focus on the job," Vyra replied. "You did everything you could. If your sister had cooperated with you, this all could have gone very differently."

"Yes, precisely," Rumér replied. "That's why we're here now, and why she *wasn't* supposed to begin this conversation with a threat to kill you, isn't that right, Your Majesty?"

Janashta grunted. "Whatever. I'm here, nobody is dead. Well, except Mother, but to be honest, she didn't have long left anyway. Whoever cursed her was speeding up the inevitable. I'm not concerned with her right now."

"Not even with who killed her?" Tashi asked.

"That is still being sorted, and frankly no longer your concern."

"What about Safir? I'd like to know what I can about her death."

Huffing impatiently, Janashta replied, "The culprit responsible for impregnating and ultimately killing her has been arrested. Her body will be exhumed from your little hiding spot and given a proper burial."

How…anticlimactic on every front. Safir deserved better than the miserable fate she'd received, but what could Tashi do? Nothing, except move on with his own life. "So what does concern you, since dead family clearly doesn't?"

"I'm concerned with getting you out of my way again." She gestured sharply to the stuffy-looking official Tashi had almost completely forgotten about, who stepped up to the table, sat down in the sole empty chair remaining, and pulled a stack of papers from a leather satchel, along with pens and ink.

It wasn't hard to guess what Janashta wanted. "So I'm signing away everything once and for all?"

"Yes, as Mother should have done to begin with."

Tashi laughed bitterly. "Mother threw me out with *nothing* but the clothes I wore. She didn't make me sign papers because she didn't think I'd survive the week." She'd probably thought he'd be dead within a day. If not for his vindictive determination to live, she might have been right.

Janashta gave him a look, the closest to respect and understanding that he'd ever seen from her. "Mother didn't know you very well, then. For what it's worth, until recently, I always believed she'd sent you overseas. I never had any reason to doubt her word, until I learned the truth a few years ago, and even then, we could not find you. I didn't know until Rumér got involved that you'd been right under my nose the whole damned time."

"What a mess, and entirely of mother's making. So fine, I'll sign your stupid papers. Gladly. But I'm not doing it for free, Your Majesty. What do I get in return, after a lifetime of abuse and being left for dead and falsely accused of murder?"

Janashta's mouth pressed into a thin line, but at Rumér's gentle nudging, she pried it open and said, "Name your price, and we'll go from there."

That was a *great* deal more than he'd expected. He looked to Vyra and Ezhil, but they only nodded in a way that said they would trust the decision to him. Tashi wasn't certain he deserved that much faith, but he'd do his best by it.

Chapter Seventeen

"First and foremost, you're going to help the Rotter. The whole city relies on them, but treats them like garbage. I don't mean you give money to someone else to fix the problem and they pocket it and nothing changes. I mean you make for actual fucking certain people are helped, like you and Mother and Grandmother and so forth should have been doing this whole time."

"Fine," Janashta said. "That's easy enough. What else? You must want something that's not all 'help the poor'."

Tashi narrowed his eyes at her, but only said, "I keep my magic, for a start."

Janashta stared at him for several long seconds, before saying, "I don't like it, but frankly taking your magic away is even more work. So be it, but if I so much as hear a whisper of your causing trouble with it, I will have it sealed away. Agreed?"

"Agreed."

"What else, then?"

"A home. Not something in the city, neither of us wants me there. Not some manor house I can't afford to keep up. A good home with plenty of land, comfortable for the three of us, with room for any guests or family we might have come visit or stay. Funds enough to keep us until we can stand on our own. Don't try to fuss or quibble, everyone in this room knows that's purse change to you."

"Anything else?" Janashta bit out, clearly reaching the end of her patience.

Tashi absolutely did not care. "Yes, actually. This place. The surrounding land. It would make a good proper traveler's point, and I have the perfect owners in mind. Also make certain we can remain here comfortably until our new home is arranged."

"Fine," Janashta said, and at his clear surprise said, "Please, it's purse change, like you said, and I know you could have asked for a whole lot more than your magic and a couple of homesteads. It will take a few days to get everything bought and signed and notarized. Do you have a particular request for your new home?"

"Somewhere with water, real water," Ezhil said. "A lake, the beach, doesn't matter. Not a dirty river nobody can touch unless they want to die of five hundred diseases at once."

Janashta snorted, looking genuinely amused for a bare moment. "Fine. It'll be done. Sign the papers. Oh, don't look at me like that. I said I'd do it, and I will. Rumér and every witness here will hold me to it."

"Leave them with me to read through and have someone retrieve them in the morning," Tashi said. "I'm not signing them blind, and I'm not going to be rushed through it. Lock me into the cabin if you're so paranoid. Like you, though, I just want this over. Have someone bring me a progress update in the morning, and I'll give you the signed papers. If I have questions, we'll discuss them tomorrow."

"Fine," Janashta replied stiffly, and rose. She hesitated, then gave a slight nod and added, "Farewell, Tashi. I hope everything goes better for you from here on. Mother should not have done what she did." She snapped her fingers and strode from the cabin with her guards and the clerk at her heels.

Rumér lingered. "She should have actually said she was sorry. For what it's worth, I really am sorry this is how everything ended. I would have liked to see you come home, Tashi. You'd be an asset and a treasure."

"The palace stopped being home a long

time ago," Tashi replied, "but thank you. If you ever want to come visit, you'd be welcome."

"I will do that," Rumér said, a bare hint of sadness in his smile. "Farewell, Tashi. All the best to you and your lovers. Gentlemen." He bowed slightly and then swept from the room, leaving them alone.

Tashi dropped back into his chair. "Well, that went better than I dared hope. I thought she'd just stab me in the heart and set the cabin on fire."

Ezhil blew out a loud breath. "Her glares alone could kill. How in the Night are you two related? She's nothing like you, except in looks."

"We used to be a lot more alike," Tashi said quietly. "I shudder to think how much worse I'd be if I'd stayed."

Vyra pulled him to his feet and into an embrace. "You killed that man for the right reasons, so I think you were already having a change of heart. Not that it matters now, since we like you exactly as you are, Your Highness."

Tashi rolled his eyes, but lifted his head to give Vyra a lingering kiss. Ezhil took a kiss of his own when they parted, and it was sorely tempting to drag them straight to bed. Instead, Tashi tore away and went to the stack of papers.

"So purely out of curiosity, what would happen if you did sign those papers and then later decided you wanted to be king, after all?" Ezhil asked as he set to work in the kitchen.

"That would take a *lot* of money. Like sums

enough even my sister would wince, because if I wanted to claim the throne, despite all the promises I wouldn't, it would require an army. Support of a great many people, especially nobles with deep pockets. Even thinking about it gives me a headache. Thankfully, it's a moot point." He sighed as he sorted through the stack of paper. "This is going to take me all night."

"Worth it, though, to be free," Vyra said. "Why did you ask for this place in addition to a home?"

Tashi looked up from the first bundle of papers. "Partly from paranoia, in case she tried to give us a really shitty property. Mostly, though, I thought your sister, or some of Ezhil's family, or both might like to have this place. All the land, the money that running a traveler station can bring in, being out of the damned Rotter… I mean, I doubt they want to abandon their restaurant, but…"

"My family is large and ever growing," Ezhil said, looking at him wide-eyed. "If you really mean it, that they could have this place… my aunts would never stop crying and thanking you."

Vyra smiled. "My sister would come, too, might even bring a couple of her friends, if Ezhil's family doesn't mind ferals, which I can't imagine they do. They'd love this spread. Could linger to help them build additional houses and buildings, maybe a proper inn, hmm? It would be a fine project. Though I admit, I'm mighty curious to see this property by the water your sister is going to buy." He laughed and shook his head. "Me, living in a proper home that the queen herself gave to me. Who would have thought."

"Do you think it will be a lake? A river? On the ocean?" Ezhil asked, wistfulness in his voice. "I always wanted to see more water than the Oss."

"Inland properties tend to be cheaper than oceanfront, but oceanfront has a higher chance of me getting killed by natural disaster," Tashi replied dryly. "So I honestly have no idea."

Ezhil laughed. "Well, the surprise will be fun, at any rate." He put the lid on the pot he'd been filling with all manner of things. "There. Dinner should be ready in a few hours."

"Damn it, I need to finish the laundry," Tashi said with a sigh. "I'll be back."

"I'll come help," Ezhil said. "I'm at loose ends until it's time for dinner."

Tashi smiled, and together they finished up the laundry in no time, leaving it to dry before scrubbing themselves clean and shuffling naked back into the cabin.

"Now there's a sight a man could grow addicted to," Vyra said from where he was finishing up remaking the bed.

Smirking, Tashi twined around him and took a kiss, heart still racing that he could do so. "To think I almost went to take care of a different job first."

"Glad you chose mine, after all," Vyra said

softly, kissing him again, hands skimming along warm, damp skin before slowly letting him go. "Come on, smells like dinner is nearly done, and you've got papers to read, much as I would love to watch Ezhil fuck you before taking a turn myself."

Tashi groaned—then hissed as Ezhil grabbed his cock while also shoving a nightshirt at him. "Stop that!"

Ezhil snickered and let go. "Suggest you read those papers quickly."

"You are the absolute worst," Tashi retorted as he pulled the shirt on before joining them at the table. Ezhil dished out soup and bread for them, and settled next to Vyra at the table, leaving the other side to Tashi and his tower of paperwork.

"Do you really understand all of that?" Ezhil asked. "I glanced at the first page, and it may as well be written in another language."

"Barely," Tashi replied. "It helps I can more or less guess what my sister is asking for: that I completely rescind my title, my claims to the throne, all family ties. Probably I won't be allowed back on palace grounds, possibly even within city limits. Might be one of the reasons she didn't quibble over my demands."

Ezhil made a face. "So you can't even come back with us to get your things? Talk to our families?"

"I'm not sure I have many 'things' worth

collecting," Tashi said. "Nothing you can't grab for me while I wait here. I have my shine and my sister's pendant—those are the only belongings I really care about. Well, more clothes would be nice, true, but soon we'll have money to get clothes properly made."

"My sister can do that. We'll buy suitable fabrics and such when we go back to the city to get her and everyone else." Vyra frowned. "Won't really be the same without you."

"Eh, probably be easier." Tashi finished off his bread and snatched another slice from the middle of the table. "Look at all the trouble I caused before we left. Not thrilled I'll be here alone for several days, but no help for it. At least I can set people on fire now."

Vyra finished his tea and pushed away from the table, eyes dark and hot as he stood. "Come set me on fire, Your Highness, before all that paperwork takes your attention for good."

"What paperwork?" Tashi muttered as he threw down what remained of his bread and nearly knocked his chair over scrambling to obey.

Vyra had settled at the edge of the bed, huge and beautiful and delightfully naked. He was idly stroking his cock, watching them with a slow-burning gaze.

It really was hard to believe how a couple of stupid jobs had led all the way to this.

"Come here," Vyra said, and Tashi complied happily, sinking to his knees in front of

Vyra, settling his hands on those lovely thighs, huge and warm, and replacing Vyra's hand with his mouth. Vyra moaned softly, fingers carding through Tashi's hair. "You're so good at that..."

The words were familiar, said any number of times by people eager to flatter a spoiled prince, or dubious-smelling clients in filthy alleyways and the rare rented-by-the-hour bed. The tone, however, was entirely new. Full of awe and admiration. Full of affection. Tashi would never get tired of it.

If this was how pleasure was supposed to be, it was no wonder people chased it so desperately. He sucked harder, taking Vyra as deep as he could, cheeks hollowing, jaw aching. There was nothing but the heat and musk, the stretch of his lips, the saliva and precome dribbling down his chin and throat.

Vyra's hand tightened in his hair, his deep groan all the warning Tashi got before Vyra was spilling down his throat. Tashi drew back as he finished swallowing, panting softly as he wiped his mouth with the back of his hand. His own cock was still hard, aching, but he left it, attention wholly on Vyra's dark, burning gaze.

Then Vyra looked up, past him, mouth curving into a faint smirk as he jerked his chin in silent command. Before Tashi could say a word, Ezhil was pressed up behind him, hands on Tashi's hips, mouth at his throat, teeth and lips working up a mark that Tashi would feel for days.

"You know what I want, pretty little prince?"

"Probably—" Tashi swore as the teeth got especially hungry. "Probably something that involves fucking me. You two seem especially fond of that."

"What can I say, you're the most beautiful person I've ever seen in my life," Ezhil said. "Even when I wanted to punch you, it was because I could not cope with how beautiful you are, even in the midst of the fucking Rotter. Beautiful and sharp and always smelling like flowers. You're even more beautiful taking a cock, and what I want is to spread out on that bed and watch as you ride me."

Tashi whimpered because he liked that idea very, *very* much.

From the rough, ragged noise that Vyra made, he also greatly approved of the idea.

Tearing away, Ezhil rose and then pulled Tashi to his feet. He climbed onto the bed, jar of lubricant with him, and settled comfortably against the pillows. Vyra kissed the side of Tashi's neck and then urged him onto the bed as well.

Tashi straddled Ezhil, teasingly stroking his cock, lost in the look on his face, the heat in those mischievous eyes.

It was Vyra's fingers, warm and slick, that pushed into him though. Not that Tashi needed much in the way of prep, given how thoroughly they'd both already had him.

"Beautiful," Ezhil said, the heated, focused

look on his face banishing whatever ability to think Tashi had remaining.

Vyra's fingers slid from his body, and he kissed the mark Ezhil had left on his throat before saying, "All ready, Your Highness." He didn't withdraw, though, only kept his hands on Tashi's hips, guiding him as he slowly sank down on Ezhil's cock.

"Fuck," Tashi said, chest heaving with the exertion and overwhelming heat of it all. He still could not get over the fact he was here with Ezhil, spread across his lap, stuffed full of his cock, body trembling with the effort to not move while Vyra's hands rested heavy on him, offering more in the way of delightful torment than needed help. Why was it so hot he was guiding Tashi as he finally started to move, lifting up before grinding back down, taking Ezhil deep. "Fuck, fuck, fuck." His head fell back as he sank entirely into sensation. The stretch of Ezhil's cock, the heat of Vyra's body, all the hands roaming over his body, every ragged compliment raining down on him.

He was more than happy to let them have him, Vyra all but controlling his movements, Ezhil touching and fondling, all their panting breaths filling the room. Tashi had been used for pleasure before, but never like this, never in a way that made him feel like he was the center of it all, that all this pleasure was for him. He didn't feel like a prince, he felt like a fucking king.

Ezhil grabbed tightly to his hips right over

Vyra's hands and fucked up into him hard and deep before shuddering, his cry of release drowning out every other sound in the room. Vyra's hand wrapped around Tashi's cock and that was all it took to finally tip him over the edge, spilling hot and sticky across Vyra's hand, leaving it to drip onto Ezhil's skin.

Groaning, Tashi pulled off Ezhil's cock and flopped down beside him on the bed. "How in the Night am I supposed to have the energy for legal paperwork now?"

"Take a short nap," Vyra said, kissing him softly before heaving out of the bed. "I'll get everything cleaned up from dinner, wake you up in an hour or two. We'll sit with you and help as we can. It's the least we can do, given what you're signing away."

"I haven't been a prince in a long time, and it never suited me, not really," Tashi replied.

Ezhil snorted as he dragged Tashi in close and kissed his brow. "Yes, it did, and king would suit you even more, but we like having you all to ourselves. Now rest, Your Highness, and after the paperwork is done, I'll reward you handsomely."

On that delightful note, Tashi was more than happy to take the ordered nap.

When he was shaken awake sometime later, flames were crackling in the fireplace, something smelled like baking apples, and Vyra was smiling down affectionately at him. "Come on, my prince, your paperwork awaits."

Tashi groaned but let Vyra drag him out of bed, soothed by the warm, lingering kiss he got once he was on his feet. He shuffled over to the table, where he got another kiss from Ezhil as he set down a pot of tea and three mugs. "You two don't have to sit with me. You must be tired, given you stayed up while I slept."

"We weren't recently sick and using a lot of powerful magic the past few days," Vyra said as he took a seat next to Tashi. "So tell me about what you're reading through as you work, if you're able. It would be interesting to hear it all."

So Tashi did, working through the papers steadily, initialing every page, and next to each full signature leaving his thumbprint in blood. By the time he was finished, his thumb was throbbing and the sun was just barely coming up, but the work was done.

He was officially, once and for all, just an ordinary person. No titles. No ties to the throne. Not even a last name. He was just Tashi. "I guess there's no point in going to bed since I'm sure…" Tashi stopped as he heard horses outside. "Seriously? She couldn't wait until a reasonable hour?"

Ezhil strode across the room and yanked the door open. A moment later, the clerk from before stepped inside. Ezhil peered out of the door. "What's with the carts?"

Tashi rose to see for himself, but Vyra waved him to sit back down as the clerk joined them.

"Good Morning, Master Tashi," the clerk replied. "I take it you found the papers in order?"

"Quite. Did my sister make you camp out until sunrise?"

The clerk's mouth twitched the barest bit. "We had a very busy night, and truly did just arrive. I didn't think you'd already be awake as well. It works out, though, since we can finish this up and find our beds that much sooner."

Tashi waved him on, pushing the stack of signed papers across the table.

In return, the clerk pushed a much smaller stack of papers across. "Your new, official identity. We didn't have a surname, so took a liberty. You can always change it at the local courts of your new home. Bank information, where you'll receive a monthly stipend for the next ten years, with an additional large deposit already made to get you started. We took the liberty of adding your lovers' names to the account as well."

"Thank you," Tashi said, glancing over the paperwork to make certain all was in order, nearly passing out at the sum of the deposit and the monthly stipend. This was much, much more than he'd expected Janashta to give him. "The house? This property?"

"This property will take a bit to secure. There seems to be some confusion and debate as to the actual owners," the clerk replied. "Nevertheless, the matter will be sorted in due course. Your new house is in progress, and the paperwork will likely be ready for signing by the end of the week. I assume you want all three names listed as owners?"

"Yes."

The clerk jotted a note on the pad of paper he'd pulled out. "We took the liberty of securing your belongings from your abode."

"The neighbors must have loved that," Tashi muttered. "What about Vyra's sister? Ezhil's family?"

"They're fine, from reports I've received. I have not spoken to anyone personally, but official letters will be hand-delivered by end of day, along with means to contact all of you," the clerk replied. "You are not allowed within the city limits, but your companions may go visit family and arrange whatever they please. There are also some gifts for you from Master Rumér, part of the trunks outside. He also arranged the other goods, thinking you could use them while you wait to settle into your new home. Any questions?"

"Where is this new home located?"

The clerk cracked a smile as he said, "An old farm estate on the edge of Lake Ressanti. I had no papers I could bring you, unfortunately, but it's a solid estate on fifty helarks. There used to be orchards there, and I believe the previous owners tended dairy cows, but that was some twenty years ago, and the property has been dormant since. There's the house, a barn, a shed, and a boathouse. Along with the orchards, there was a private garden, but I can only imagine the state it's in now."

Tashi's head was spinning, and he didn't need to look to know his lovers were just as knocked over. "Sounds perfect, thank you. Who should I contact and how if we have further questions?"

"Me, and you can do it via means magical or mundane." He set a small, silver charm on top of the papers. An echo, it was called, costly magic that allowed instant communication between two points.

Tashi scooped it up and tucked it away in a pocket. "Thank you, I think that's everything." He looked to the other two, who shook their heads.

The clerk rose, gathering up the stack of papers Tashi had signed. "Excellent. I will see you again when the rest of the paperwork is ready for signing. Good day to you all."

When he was gone, Tashi pushed the papers across to the other two. "There's a bank account right now with ten thousand rils waiting for us to use. I get a stipend of one thousand rils a month, starting next month, for the next ten years. After that, we're on our own."

"A thousand *rils*. A *month*. My family on its busiest months doesn't make a *hundred* rils, Tashi." Ezhil fell into chair. "Ten thousand just sitting there." He looked on the verge of crying, and nearby Vyra looked the same.

"A lot more than I expected from her, not going to lie," Tashi said. "That deposit alone more than covered her end of that part of the bargain, but the stipend… Well, if we're smart and careful, we won't have to worry about anything else ever again. Especially since we already have a home, and this place should we ever need it, though hopefully we can leave it to your relatives and never have to trouble them."

Vyra kissed him, pulling him out of his chair and nearly right off his feet, one hand in his hair and the other around his waist. "You're wonderful, Tashi."

Tashi laughed. "I'm not any such thing, but you're welcome to keep thinking so. Glad I've proven good for something. I'm just happy we're out of the fucking Rotter."

"I'm happy your demands included *helping* the Rotter," Ezhil said. "I wonder if she really will."

"She will, or Rumér will make her life miserable." Tashi smiled. "He has a lot of power over her now, and they both know it. He never wanted to be Warlock Prime, but I suspect that's what he'll do now. Glad it's not my problem."

"You would have made a fine Warlock Prime, but I'm happy you're here with us, Your Highness," Ezhil said, sliding in as they shifted to make room for him. "Shall we have apple dumplings for breakfast and then sleep the rest of the day like a bunch of decadent spoiled brats?"

Tashi laughed, holding them tightly, so happy he might just cry. "That sounds perfect."

Fin

Epilogue

Two years later

"Where's Ezhil?" Tashi asked as he set down the apples he'd brought from the east orchard, wiping sweat from his brow with his shirt sleeve but really only adding dirt to the mess.

Vyra snorted, not looking up from the meat he was preparing for smoking. "Where do you think?"

Tashi rolled his eyes, but his mouth curved into a smile. The first thing Ezhil did the moment his chores were done was go for a swim, out to the tiny little scrub of island in the middle of the lake and back. He'd practically become a fish from the moment of their arrival.

"How's the harvesting?" Vyra asked, snagging Tashi as he passed and tugging him into a quick kiss.

"Nearly done. Shouldn't take more than a couple of hours tomorrow morning to finish up." Once the apples were harvested, they were finished for the year. Most of the apples would be sold, but they always kept some to turn into various goods for their own pantry: dried, jams and jellies, cider, vinegar, and more.

They'd expected not much of anything when they'd finally reached their new home, but had found that the long-abandoned orchards were doing rather well. Cleaning them up, getting rid of the dead trees and such had taken most of a year, but now they had three whole functioning orchards: peaches, pears, and apples. Their respective harvest times were spread out perfectly, providing fruit to sell and use throughout the year. Between the orchards, the extensive gardens Ezhil maintained, and the animals that fell under Vyra's care, they had a solid homestead with plenty of additional income.

It was a better life than Tashi had ever imagined he could have, including the royal one he'd signed away for good.

Tashi washed up and pulled on clean clothes, then pulled up a stool and set to washing and sorting the apples, listening to Vyra's humming and singing as he worked.

By the time he had the apples ready for

their various fates, which he'd start tackling in the morning, since dark was rapidly falling now, Vyra had finished his task as well. The meat would smoke through the night and be ready for hanging in the morning. Winter was still a couple of months away, plenty of time to finish up their stocking.

He'd just finished cleaning up and changing into lounging clothes when Ezhil reappeared, damp and smelling of the honey flower soap Tashi had purchased on their last trip into town. "Hello, darlings."

Tashi laughed. "Ezhil. How was the lake?"

"Still nice and warm. Some of the winter fish are starting to wake, be good eating soon. Did the post come today?"

Vyra nodded to the table, not pausing in his work dishing out their dinner, a fragrant soup that had been quietly simmering all day, using up some vegetables that wouldn't keep much longer. "Haven't had a chance to look it through, but I think something came from your aunt."

"Finally!" Ezhil said, and dug through the small pile of letters, bills, and a couple of packages that should be the fabric samples Tashi had ordered and some seeds Ezhil had wanted for the herb garden. Locating the letter he was seeking, Ezhil tore it open and read in silence for a moment. "They can come! Auntie was able to hire and train up people to watch the inn while she and the others come to see us! Hooray!"

Tashi smiled. "Can't believe we're finally going to have visitors. I guess I need to finish up the spare quilt, and *you* need to finish building the new beds. The hands and our pending guests deserve better than the creaky monstrosities currently in there."

Ezhil laughed and kissed him, then Vyra, before snagging a piece of the bread that Vyra had just placed on the table. "I'll get it done, especially now the cold is starting to come in, and my garden won't last too much longer." They had a winter garden, but mostly they got by on stores. The first year had been difficult as they learned to live a life very different from that in the Rotter, but thanks to the bargain he'd made, they were never truly in danger of starving to death or being homeless.

Never again.

Tashi took his seat at the table and slathered a piece of bread with butter Ezhil had made that morning. He took a large bite, then used the rest of the slice to dip in his soup between bites. "This is delicious."

Ezhil grinned, pleased as always at how much his cooking was appreciated. Tashi and Vyra did most of the gathering and preserving; Ezhil did most of the cooking and maintained their gardens. Once every couple of weeks they went into town to buy what they couldn't make, and every few days during harvests purchasers came for their fruit.

They hadn't really needed his sister's

stipend for some time, but Tashi kept it anyway, letting the money build, an emergency fund should something go wrong.

The house had needed a lot of work when they'd first arrived, even more rundown than they'd feared, but they'd had the money and the time, and people in town were happy to have the work. Now they had a sprawling farmhouse: three bedrooms that were used by the workers they hired to help with the harvest, the kitchen and dining area, a sitting room with plenty of space, a sewing room for him, a workshop for Ezhil and Vyra, the enormous pantry, and up in the loft area was their master bedroom, probably the most luxurious and ridiculous thing he'd ever had to his name since being cast out onto the streets.

Outside were the vegetable garden, the herb garden, and most recently, an area Ezhil was clearing to make room for tea and flowers come spring. There was the fishing boat, the orchards, the cows, chickens, and goats, and they were hoping to add ducks and geese soon.

They'd have to hire some permanent hands too, but that was another matter that would keep until spring.

When they'd finished supper, Tashi cleaned up the table, while Vyra and Ezhil tackled the dishes, and gave everything a quick sweep when they were done. Lighting the lamps around the house, he fetched the quilt pieces he was working on from the basket in his sewing room and settled on the long sofa in front of the fire to work. Ezhil settled in the armchair that was probably his favorite object in the whole house, and Vyra on the stool he used while doing his woodworking.

They worked, chatting idly, until conversation became mostly yawns and the fancy clock Ezhil had insisted on chimed it was ten o'clock. Horrendously early if they still lived in the city, especially for body catchers, but now it almost felt like they were going to bed a little late.

Tashi climbed into bed first, stretching out in the middle that had somehow become his spot. He certainly wasn't complaining, especially not when the other two decided it wasn't quite time to go to sleep after all.

Though it would be their fault entirely when he was a bit slow to get to work in the morning.

Fin

About the Author

Megan is a long-time resident of queer romance and keeps herself busy reading and writing it. She is often accused of fluff and nonsense. When she's not involved in writing, she likes to cook, harass her wife and cats, or watch movies. She loves to hear from readers and can be found all over the internet.

meganderr.com
patreon.com/meganderr
meganderr.blogspot.com
facebook.com/meganaprilderr
meganaderr@gmail.com
@meganaderr